MW00942724

STORIES *from* MY FATHER'S BARBERSHOP

JOE DAVID GARNER JR.

iUniverse, Inc.
Bloomington

Stories from My Father's Barbershop

Copyright © 2012 by Joe David Garner Jr.

All rights reserved. No part of this book may be used or reproduced by any means, graphic, electronic, or mechanical, including photocopying, recording, taping or by any information storage retrieval system without the written permission of the publisher except in the case of brief quotations embodied in critical articles and reviews.

Certain characters in this work are historical figures, and certain events portrayed did take place. However, this is a work of fiction. All of the other characters, names, and events as well as all places, incidents, organizations, and dialogue in this novel are either the products of the author's imagination or are used fictitiously.

iUniverse books may be ordered through booksellers or by contacting:

iUniverse
1663 Liberty Drive
Bloomington, IN 47403
www.iuniverse.com
1-800-Authors (1-800-288-4677)

Because of the dynamic nature of the Internet, any web addresses or links contained in this book may have changed since publication and may no longer be valid. The views expressed in this work are solely those of the author and do not necessarily reflect the views of the publisher, and the publisher hereby disclaims any responsibility for them.

Any people depicted in stock imagery provided by Thinkstock are models, and such images are being used for illustrative purposes only.
Certain stock imagery © Thinkstock.

ISBN: 978-1-4759-2242-4 (sc)
ISBN: 978-1-4759-2243-1 (ebk)

Printed in the United States of America

iUniverse rev. date: 06/04/2012

CONTENTS

PREFACE

While serving in the army during World War II, my father took advantage of every opportunity to learn a new skill. He took a barber's training course, obtained a barber's license, and opened his own shop after leaving the army in 1946. It was a small shop with only one chair, and it was constructed under the shade of the big oak tree in our yard. The front area of the shop had milk crates for sitting and for playing checkers. I was not allowed to "hang around" the shop very much until I was about ten years old, when my father and the older men who hung around the shop felt I could appreciate some of the stories they had to share. The core group of about six regular storytellers was from sixty-five to ninety years of age. I never knew if any of their stories, or the information about the lives of the storytellers, was true, but I found some of them very entertaining. I decided to share some of my favorites.

ACKNOWLEDGMENTS

It is not possible for me to say thank-you to every person who has been a positive influence, a supporter, and a lifeline throughout my life. However, I can assure you that without each and every one of them, this book would not have been possible, nor would anything else I have achieved in my life. I want to express my heartfelt thanks and appreciation for all of them, past and present, and I know there will be others in the future. My life is a living testimony that it not only takes a village to raise a child, but that village must continue to expand if a person is to have the possibility of maximizing his or her potential for growth and productivity. God has and continues to provide me with bountiful blessings from all of you. I am still compelled to express a special thank-you to my parents, Joe David Garner Sr. and Brunetta Hyman-Garner; my grandparents, Ed Garner Sr. and Hennie Williams-Garner, Willie Hyman and Mollie Johnson-Hyman; Thomas Douglas, my college English professor who encouraged me to write, and who, after reading my first short story, told me that I must continue to write; Robert Disch and Harry "Rick" Moody, coworkers at Hunter College, who helped me get one of my stories published; and last but not least, my wife of twenty-five years, Tramel, and my son, Jared, who both allowed and encouraged whatever I needed to do to complete this project. Again, I thank you all.

CHAPTER 1

THE DORIS HOLLY STORY

It was my family's tradition to attend Sunday school and church service every Sunday starting at 10:00 a.m. My father would open his barbershop from 6:00 a.m. to 8:00 a.m. on Sundays to accommodate preachers and church deacons who wanted to look their best on Sunday mornings, especially the "jackleg" (untrained and unlicensed) preachers and other church leaders who had spent Saturday night at Ms. Holly's house. Matthew "Preacher" Casey was considered one of the more respectable "jackleg" preachers because he always conducted himself appropriately in public and never spent the entire night at Ms. Holly's house. Preacher Casey said that he was eighty-two years old, but he wasn't exactly sure because he was born at home, and no one in his family could read or write. A few days after his birth, a traveling preacher came to his home and was able to write a few words in a Bible about his birth and give it to his mother. The traveling preacher told his mother that something about Matthew's eyes told him that Matthew would someday be a preacher. Preacher Casey had an amazingly strong voice for a man eighty-two years old, five feet five, and 125 pounds.

One Sunday morning in August 1958, he talked about the "heart-to-heart" talk he had with Ms. Holly and the high regard he had for her at the end of their talk.

Doris Holly was born in Sandstone, Mississippi, a small town of about three hundred fifty located thirty five miles northwest of Crest Ridge, Mississippi, on February 8, 1908. Her parents, Clifford and Nellie Holly, were both Crest Ridge city maintenance workers. They were part of the staff that cleaned the inside of city buildings such as city hall, the courthouse, the fire department, and the police station. Doris was two years older than her younger sister, Debra. In 1958 Doris was fifty years old and had started making money for herself in 1926 when she and Debra formed a partnership with their uncle Zeke to help him sell his moonshine. She was five feet six and weighed 115 pounds. Both her parents, who were Negro, had one parent of Cajun descent. Doris and her sister Debra, who was five feet seven and weighed 120 pounds, had smooth, unblemished olive skin with shoulder-length, curly, jet-black hair. Their eyes were brown but at first glance seemed to be black, which made them look very Cajun rather than white.

Doris's parents were hard workers and tried to provide the best care and life possible for her and her sister. They lived in a small two-bedroom home in Sandstone that her parents rented for ten dollars a month from Dean Holland, a Crest Ridge furniture store owner. The girls were very fortunate that their parents worked for the city of Crest Ridge and were respected by city officials who knew them, which enabled Doris and Debra to attend the schools in Crest Ridge and receive their high school diplomas. Doris was impressed by all the important city officials who were also major business owners. She and Debra talked a lot about what kind of life they wanted for themselves and agreed that it would take money to rise above the usual jobs that Negroes were able to get. They also agreed that they did not want to be subject to the kind of sexual abuse that most Negro women viewed as something they just had to accept from men. Doris and Debra knew that having enough money to buy the protection they needed from sexual abuse was the only way they could keep themselves safe. They also knew that it was extremely difficult for women to own businesses similar to those owned by men in Crest Ridge. What seemed obvious was that the most money made by Negroes came from bootleg alcohol, gambling, and prostitution. The most successful Negro they had heard their parents and other adults talk about was the Prince of Pleasure, whose real name was Rufus Jones. Doris learned how to make moonshine and wine from her uncle Zeke Holly, who was a day laborer and spent his nights making and selling moonshine and wine. Uncle Zeke probably drank more of his moonshine than he sold. Doris's goal was to make as much money as possible, so she decided to find out as much as she could about how Rufus Jones became so successful. She concluded that there were a few important requirements: an environment that was comfortable, private, and well maintained; high quality in what was available and provided to customers; and attracting people with money, especially successful men, to come to your place of business. Doris and Debra agreed that they would need to start small and grow their business. Their most difficult first step was to break the news to their parents about their plan. The most important thing that she and Debra stressed to their parents was that they did not want to become victims of the usual life of Negroes. They knew that there were risks involved in what they wanted to do, but the risks that Negroes faced every day were just as great and dangerous. At least their plan might give them an opportunity to escape the certain dangers that would befall them as they do for almost all Negroes. Their parents did not agree with what they wanted to do, but they made it clear that they would always love them and they should never be afraid to come home if their plan failed.

In June 1926, Doris and Debra went to their uncle Zeke and convinced him to let them sell some of his moonshine and wine, and they would give him half of the money they made. Uncle Zeke agreed. Doris's first idea, which seemed to her to be a factor in Rufus Jones's success, worked immediately, which was that men would buy more alcohol from a pretty girl than they would from a half-drunk older man. She and Debra cleaned up Uncle Zeke's kitchen and his back porch and set up three small tables that could seat four people each. At fifty cents a pint, Doris and Debra sold all the moonshine and wine Uncle Zeke could make. Doris then convinced Uncle Zeke to build another still so she could help him make more moonshine. The word was spreading about Doris and Debra being the beautiful hostesses at Zeke's house and being available to bring special orders to customers' locations if necessary. Doris and Debra agreed that they would not have sex with the men no matter what they offered. They did not want anything like pregnancy or illness to stop them from making money.

In June of 1927, their moonshine and wine business had grown to four stills, and the increased business and profits motivated their uncle Zeke to sober up and become a better partner in the business. Uncle Zeke's increased attention to and improvement of the stilling process created a higher-quality-tasting moonshine. He actually started to demonstrate pride in his work. The extra money enabled improvements to be made to Uncle Zeke's home, and the entire first floor was converted to resemble a hotel lobby with a bar and lounge area for group sitting and private booths.

Doris and Debra realized that with the improvements to Uncle Zeke's home, they would need more attractive girls to work the bar and serve in the lounge area. Doris, Debra, and Uncle Zeke decided not to allow anyone else near the stills to avoid mistakes and deliberate tampering. Doris and Debra were very careful in their selection of the girls to work in the bar and lounge. In addition to beauty, they selected five women from age eighteen to thirty-five as some of their male customers preferred to be served by more mature women.

Things went well for Doris, Debra, and their uncle Zeke selling quality moonshine and wine. By March 1, 1928, they had tucked away at least $3,000 for a rainy day in addition to sharing the weekly profits after paying the five women who were working in the bar and lounge. On March 10, 1928, they had an unexpected customer, Danmore Blackberry, Crest Ridge's best semiprofessional baseball player. None of them was aware that Mr. Blackberry knew they existed or how to find them. Mr. Blackberry walked up to the bar and asked to speak with the owner. Doris saw Mr. Blackberry walk in and was at the bar in time to respond to his question.

"Good afternoon, Mr. Blackberry. I am one of the owners. My name is Doris Holly."

"Well, Ms. Holly, I'm glad to know that you know who I am, and I want to say that I am glad that I now know who you are. I won't waste your valuable time, so I will come right to the point. The Crest Ridge baseball team is preparing for a St. Patrick's Day party on March 15, and several of the men on the team have heard that you have the best moonshine and homemade wine in Crest Ridge. If possible, I would like to buy a gallon of moonshine and two gallons of wine for the party, and I would personally like to buy a quart of wine to take home with me tonight."

"It would be my pleasure to provide you and your guests with some of my very best moonshine and homemade wine, Mr. Blackberry. I would also like to give you—free of charge—a quart of wine for you and your wife to enjoy tonight."

"Audrey, I'll watch the bar while you go to my office and get a bottle of wine for Mr. Blackberry."

"Mr. Blackberry, that will be a total of twelve dollars for the moonshine and wine."

"Ms. Holly, I am sure that I will consider twelve dollars a bargain if your moonshine and wine are half as good as I have been told. I will send my driver, James, on the morning of the fifteenth for the moonshine and wine."

"It will be ready and waiting for him, Mr. Blackberry. I hope you will come again soon."

After their party on March 15, Mr. Blackberry and several other baseball players started to show up with their drivers on a regular basis, buying both moonshine and wine. The business started another level of growth.

On April 12, 1928, Doris received a letter from her maternal aunt, Mable Sheppard, in Dust Creek, Mississippi. The letter was written by Mable's husband, Jeffery, who said that Mable was very ill and needed to have a hernia operation, but they had no money to pay for the surgery. Mable was her mother's older sister by ten years. Mable was fifty years old, and Jeffery was sixty-five. Ms. Holly wrote back to her uncle Jeffery and told him that she would pay for the surgery regardless of the cost, and he should tell Mable's doctor to schedule the surgery as soon as possible. Doris also wrote that she would stay and care for Aunt Mable after the surgery.

It took Doris two days to get things in order with Debra and Uncle Zeke because she told them she did not know how long she would be away taking care of Aunt Mable. Debra offered to come with her, but Doris insisted that Debra remain to help Uncle Zeke with the business. When Doris arrived in Dust Creek in the home of her aunt Mable and uncle Jeffery, she realized that much needed to be done to ensure that Mable would have a good recovery at home. At five feet tall and one hundred pounds, Aunt Mable had been a domestic worker since the age of fourteen and had not been feeling well for the last two years because of her hernia condition. Uncle Jeffery was five feet eight and weighed 175 pounds. He was physically able at sixty-five to still do day labor, which he had done for the last forty years, but was never able to handle emotional issues when they affected anyone close to him. When problems arose he turned to Mable for support. Her illness caused him to not eat or sleep properly. They lived very poorly, just managing to pay their bills and buy enough food to keep them going. They knew about Doris, Debra, and Zeke's financial success from the letters they received from Nellie, Doris and Debra's mother, but they never told Nellie about their severe financial problems or Mable's hernia.

Mable made it through the surgery, but the doctor told Doris that she would need good care at home to make a full recovery. Doris told the doctor that she would make sure her aunt Mable received the best of care.

The day before Mable was discharged from the hospital, Doris went to the grocery store and bought sufficient good food to last the entire week. She started right away cooking vegetables, cornbread, and fried chicken. Since Mable's illness, Jeffery had become sick with worry and was not able to work. Doris was determined to nourish them both back to good health. When Mable returned home she was very weak, much weaker than Doris thought she would be. She forced them both to eat the food she prepared daily and drink juices and milk in addition to water.

What began as an emergency trip to help a sick aunt and uncle turned into a two-year stay that then turned into a permanent relocation. In February 1931, Doris wrote to Debra and her parents to tell them that her aunt and uncle's lives depended on the provision of good care and treatment, and since they had no children to care for them, she could not have peace of mind putting such a responsibility in the hands of a paid nonfamily member. Doris wrote to Debra and told her that the Negroes had no quality place to go for entertainment like the one they created. She asked Debra if she could hire a

STORIES FROM MY FATHER'S BARBERSHOP

couple of men to help her bring the equipment and supplies for two stills, which she would build in the wooded section of Aunt Mable and Uncle Jeffery's backyard. Their backyard was perfect for the stills and a private entrance. They also had a large enough front and side yard to add a section to the house, complete with a modest bedroom, kitchen, dining room, living room, and full bathroom. The new section of the house would also serve as the front entrance. The new section of the house would be exclusively for Aunt Mable and Uncle Jeffery and would face the main access road. No customers would enter or have access to the new section of the house.

After receiving Doris's letter, Debra arrived three days later with everything her sister needed—and the $3,000 they and Uncle Zeke had initially saved—to help get her started. Debra told her that if she needed more money to let her know.

Doris not only duplicated the alcohol business she, her sister, and Uncle Zeke built in Crest Ridge, she added gambling and prostitution. The addition of gambling and prostitution started with the card games, especially poker and blackjack. The men would play all night long, or at least as long as they had money in their pockets. They would also drink all night long, which caused them to leave her house drunk. To keep the men from drawing too much attention to the house by leaving drunk, she added a third floor to the house and made it into four bedrooms so the men could get some sleep before leaving. She also had four bedrooms on the second floor; three were used for gambling, primarily card games, and one for dice. She had a bedroom for herself build in the backyard directly in front of the stills. Every person utilizing a room on the second or third floor paid her three dollars, and the winners of the card and dice games had to give her 10 percent of the jackpot. Because of the four very beautiful eighteen to thirty-year-old girls she hired to be hostesses and serve drinks, the men began to offer her money to allow them to have sex with them. The girls also pleaded with Doris to agree because they needed the extra money. Doris resisted at first because she did not like the idea of women being taken advantage of by men, but she finally gave in and made the rooms on the third floor rentals for hourly or nightly rates—fifty cents per hour or three dollars per night. They would also have to pay five dollars directly to the girls. On the first-floor bar and lounge area, moonshine was ten cents a shot, and wine was ten cents per six-ounce glass. Ms. Holly said the men were usually able to keep each other under control, but when the prostitution started she had to hire three men, one stationed on each floor, to serve as security enforcers. They were told to protect the girls, to make sure no one accidentally opened the curtain that led to Aunt Mable and Uncle Jeffery's section of the house, and to use good judgment and let the men settle their own differences when possible.

Ms. Holly became one of the most successful businesswomen in the state of Mississippi. What was not generally known was that she was one of the most God-fearing persons in the state and the biggest financial contributor to the Greater Heaven Baptist Church in Dust Creek. She paid the entire cost for the new roof on the church, and bought new choir robes and hymnals and the pastor's new car and robe.

CHAPTER 2

THE STORY OF THE "BIG FIGHT"

On April 20, 1970, old Jacob "Mulehead" McCain told the story of the "Big Fight." Mulehead was about eighty years old, about five feet nine, with a firm, strong, dark-skinned body developed during a lifelong career as a sharecropper, and he seemed to know every person over the age of forty, both black and white, in the entire town by name.

Every Friday about 5:00 p.m. down at Ms. Holly's, the weekend poker games started, and sometimes a game would last until early Monday morning.

On Friday night, April 16, 1948, about 10:00 p.m., Bender Giles, Morris John Thomas, Ralph Henson, and Jerry "Junior" Samuels arrived minutes apart and decided to start a new poker game. Their game began drawing to a close around 11:30 p.m. on Saturday night when Morris John bet and lost his last five dollars of the $350 he started with and Junior Samuels lost his last dollar from the $365 he had when the game started. Bender had been winning big for the previous three hours, and Ralph had been losing heavily for the previous six hours. As a last-chance effort to win back the $400 he had lost, Ralph bet his 1947 Ford.

"Ralph, put your car keys in your pocket and get out of the game, because if you lose the bet you won't get your car back."

"Bender, I been playing poker a long time, and I know the rules, and I don't need you to tell them to me! I also know that if I win this next bet I will get most of my money back. You play your cards, and I'll play mine."

Ralph actually had a good hand, a full house—three tens and two queens. However, Bender had that rare king of all poker hands, a royal flush. Bender reached for Ralph's car keys, which were on the poker table with the money. Ralph managed to grab the keys before Bender could reach them and stood up from the table.

"Give me the keys, Ralph."

"Shut up, Bender, and take the money you won and go home."

Ralph was twenty-seven years old, six feet one, and about 210 pounds. Bender was thirty-five years old, six feet five, and about 240 pounds. Everyone, especially Bender, knew that if he did not get Ralph's car keys, he would never be respected in the game again. Ralph knew that his wife would leave him if he came home without the car. That would be the final straw for her trying to deal with his gambling problem.

"Ralph, you got ten seconds to give me those keys."

"Bender, the only way you getting my car keys is to kill me."

Bender didn't want to hurt Ralph, but he had to get those keys, so he got up from the table and slapped Ralph across his face with his open hand.

"Boy, don't make me kill you; give me those keys."

Ralph punched Bender in the stomach. This angered Bender, and he hit Ralph in the jaw hard enough to knock him out of the room and into the hallway. Ralph attempted to get up, but Bender came out of the room and hit him in the jaw again as he was trying to get up. When Ralph fell back to the floor again, Bender tried to get the car keys from his pocket. Ralph recovered enough to turn and punch Bender in the left ear. The blow was hard enough to cause Bender to grab his ear and back up. Bender found out later that his eardrum had burst. Bender then hit Ralph again in the jaw, and by the sound of the impact everyone knew Ralph's jaw was broken. Bender then hit Ralph three times in the stomach and once more in the jaw. Ralph screamed in pain and fell to his knees. Bender hit Ralph once more in the side of his head, and Ralph seemed to faint. Bender then took the keys from Ralph's pocket and started to leave Ms. Holly's house. When Bender got outside he decided to drive Ralph's car home and return later for his car. As he was about to enter Ralph's car, someone yelled, "Here comes Ralph!" Bender turned and saw Ralph coming with the baseball bat that Ms. Holly kept in the corner of the poker room.

"Don't come any closer, Ralph."

Ralph kept coming. Bender then reached into the pocket of his overalls and pulled out a .32-caliber handgun.

"Ralph, for the last time, don't come any closer."

Ralph took another step, which put him about fifteen feet from Bender. Bender then shot Ralph in the left leg. Ralph started to fall, but at the same time he threw the bat at Bender. Bender turned but could not dodge the bat, and it hit him in the small of his back. The pain caused Bender to slowly drop to the ground. Bender became so angry that he shot Ralph twice in the chest. Ralph died almost immediately.

Everyone then slowly began to leave and felt bad for both Ralph and Bender. No one was actually afraid, because they knew the police would not be interested in Negro-on-Negro crime. Bender stayed on the ground until he felt better, and he and Junior Samuels later buried Ralph in Ms. Holly's front yard. Ms. Holly was not disturbed or concerned, as there were already three other bodies buried in her front yard. Ms. Holly told Bender that she understood what had happened and that he was still welcome in her house.

CHAPTER 3

THE FRANK PERRY JR. STORY

Nathan House was born in Waterfall, Mississippi, on November 3, 1915. He was the third born of six brothers and two sisters. Unlike many of his friends, Nathan was able to stay in school until the sixth grade before he had to go to work as a day laborer on the fruit and vegetable farms along the Gulf Coast to help his parents and two older brothers support the family. It was while working with the older teenagers that he first learned about a local legend by the name of Frank Perry Jr. When Nathan first heard the story, he did not believe that much of it was true. It was the constant hearing of the story, particularly as it was told by some of the men in their twenties and thirties who said that they had known Frank Perry Jr. and other characters such as Rufus Jones, who was known as the Prince of Pleasure, that Nathan started to pay attention and then tried to learn as much as he could about Frank Perry Jr. In 1960, Nathan left the Gulf Coast to live with his sister, Betty, just outside of Crest Ridge, Mississippi, and became a regular at the barbershop. In March 1965, he told the men all he knew about the Gulf Coast legend of Frank Perry Jr.

Frank Perry Jr. was born in Waterfall, Mississippi, on June 9, 1892. Waterfall was more a community of about fifty people than a town, located about fifty miles south of Crest Ridge. Frank never knew his parents, Frank Sr. and Daisy Perry, and was raised by a paternal aunt, Glenda Perry-Smith. Aunt Glenda told him and his older sister, Shirley, that their parents died in September of 1892 during a hurricane-force storm. After placing Frank Jr. and Shirley in the basement room that Frank Sr. had dug under the floor of their living room for just such an occasion, he and Daisy tried to wedge chairs under all the doors in the house in hopes that it would add some support for the house against the high winds. Before coming back to the living room, Daisy remembered that they had no milk bottles or food for the children in the basement. She yelled to Frank Sr. that she was going to the kitchen to get a milk bottle and a few biscuits that were left from breakfast. When she got to the icebox, the wind blew a large tree limb through the kitchen window, which struck Daisy in the back and knocked her unconscious. Frank Sr. heard the sound of the window breaking in the kitchen and, as quickly as he could, climbed out of the basement room, closed the door behind him, and ran to the kitchen to get Daisy. He saw her lying on the floor under the tree limb and climbed over the limb to help her, but he could not pick Daisy up and carry her against the force of the wind. He laid her on the floor and covered her with his body. After the storm, Glenda's husband, Arthur Smith, found Daisy and Frank Sr. still on the floor in the kitchen. The force of the limb had broken Daisy's back, and she probably died before the storm ended. The continual onslaught of large debris hitting Frank Jr. caused multiple serious wounds. He never regained consciousness and died about twenty minutes after

Arthur lifted him from the floor. Frank Jr.'s sister, Shirley, who was six years old at the time, held Frank Jr. in her arms and sang songs to him during the storm. Arthur knew about the basement in the living room and found Shirley and Frank Jr. uninjured.

Glenda and Arthur raised Shirley and Frank Jr. as their own children, but always told them stories about their parents and how important it was for them to know and remember what good people they were, and that they had both sacrificed their lives for them. Fortunately, a couple of pictures of Frank Sr. and Daisy were recovered after the storm. Every June 1, Glenda and Arthur would prepare a decorated cake and have a family celebration in honor of Frank Sr. and Daisy. The family would share their memories, thoughts, and feelings about Frank Sr. and Daisy with Shirley and Frank Jr. By age twelve, Shirley began to appreciate the annual family celebration of her parents, and the event no longer made her feel just sadness. She began to feel pride in the love and respect that everyone had for her parents. She began to understand the love and commitment they had for her and her brother, and that while they surely would rather have survived the storm, the testimonies of family members made her feel certain that her parents never hesitated or regretted the decisions they made on that day, which cost them their lives. As she grew older, Shirley's pride and appreciation for her parents turned to commitment and determination to do her very best with whatever abilities God gave her. She began having private conversations with Frank Jr., telling him that they both must do the best they could to be the kind of people that would have made their parents proud. Shirley told Frank Jr. that they owed this to their parents.

In 1902, at the age of sixteen, Shirley had become a very good cook and housekeeper through Glenda's careful training and supervision. Glenda worked at a modest-size restaurant called The Road Stop as a cook. She decided to ask her boss and restaurant manager, David Green, if he would consider giving Shirley a job as dishwasher and kitchen helper. A kitchen helper was someone who did any job he or she was instructed to do, which was generally cleaning the pots and pans and the entire restaurant after closing. The restaurant already had one kitchen helper, an older black gentleman called Luke. Luke was five feet seven and weighed about 170 pounds. He seemed to be about forty or fifty years old, but no one, including Luke, knew his real age or his last name. Luke could only remember being sent from farm to farm as a child to work and to be attended to by various Negro sharecropping families. While physically very strong and strikingly muscular for a man of his age, his mind was rather weak, and he could not remember detailed instructions or information well. Luke was good-natured and friendly, and would do anything asked of him for only mild praise in return. Mr. Green's uncle, Jackson Green, owned the restaurant, which he opened in 1890. On a morning in 1897, when Jackson Green came to open the restaurant, he found Luke sitting on the steps of the restaurant.

"Hey, boy, why you sitting here?"

"Well, sur, I was traveling in a wagon with a family, and we wuz all going to find work. We stopped last night under that big tree over yonder to eat supper and then we all went to sleep. When I woke up this mon'in, they wuz gone, and I don't know whare they went."

"What's your name, boy?"

"My name's Luke, sur."

"Are you hungry, Luke?"

"Luke is real hungry, sur."

"If I give you food, Luke, you are going to have to do some work for me to pay for what you eat."

"Sur, the only thing Luke likes more than eating is working."

Mr. Green did not know if Luke was giving an accurate account of what had happened to him, but he could tell that Luke was mentally very slow. Mr. Green believed that Luke was lost but felt that someone would come along soon looking for him. There was no way that Luke could survive on his own. Someone must be looking for him or would be soon.

Mr. Green told his cook, Lonnie Andrews, to fix Luke a good breakfast. Luke ate four eggs, six pancakes, eight strips of bacon, and two large glasses of milk.

"That was quite a breakfast you ate there, Luke. You ready to work now?"

"Yes, sur, Mr. Green. That was a mighty good breakfast, and Luke is ready to work."

"I'm glad to hear that, Luke. I want you to start by cleaning all the pots and pans. I want Lonnie to spend his time cooking, not washing pots and pans."

"Yes, sur, Mr. Green. Luke will make them pots and pans shine."

No one came that day to get Luke, so Mr. Green told him he could have more food if he cleaned the tables and the floor of the restaurant at the close of the day. Luke also decided to clean the pots and pans again. He cleaned the floor and the pots and pans beyond Mr. Green's expectations.

"Luke, this floor and the pots and pans haven't been this clean since I built the place a few years ago."

Mr. Green took Luke home with him and allowed him to sleep on a cot in his storage room. No one ever came for Luke, and Mr. Green's storage room became Luke's home.

Jackson Green appreciated Glenda and Luke's dependable and trustworthy hard work. He actually had more confidence in them to show up and do a good day's work than he had in his twenty-year-old daughter, Jean Ann, who worked the cash register in the restaurant, and his twenty-five-year-old son, Dixon, who was responsible for inventory and ordering supplies for the restaurant. As his nephew, David, was more reliable and had a personality better suited for dealing with the public, he selected him to be the manager of the restaurant. David told Glenda he would be willing to give Shirley an opportunity to work. However, if she did not work out after a week, he would not allow her to continue. Glenda agreed to this arrangement and explained it to Shirley. Shirley was very happy and promised Glenda that she would do her very best.

David Green also had a lot of respect for Glenda and her work ethic. She was efficient, dependable, and trustworthy.

However, Shirley's outstanding work on her first day reminded him of his uncle Jackson's description of Luke's first day of work. Shirley did every task asked of her very thoroughly, admirably, and with pride in the results. At the end of her first week, David Green told Shirley how pleased he was with her work, and he hoped she would continue to work at the restaurant.

Frank Jr. was blessed with the ability to learn very quickly. His aunt Glenda and uncle Arthur did everything they could to promote and support his learning. When Frank Jr. was six years old, Glenda would bring home newspapers from the restaurant that customers had left behind for him to read. Frank Jr. would read the newspaper aloud for his uncle Arthur, who could not read. Arthur would explain to him how the information in the newspaper affected their lives. By age ten, Frank Jr. began to ask Arthur questions about the differences in the ways that Negroes and whites were treated. Arthur could see that the more Frank Jr. learned about his life in the "Jim Crow" South, the angrier and more disillusioned he became.

In 1906, at the age of fourteen, Frank Jr. had learned all that was available to him in the segregated school he attended. His teachers had only an eighth-grade education and had limited experience and awareness of matters outside the Waterfall area. Frank Jr. told his uncle Arthur and aunt Glenda that he saw no point in continuing to go to school. His time could be better spent getting a job and earning money to help the family. Arthur and Glenda sadly agreed with his conclusion, as they had no way to provide him with any additional formal educational opportunities.

Frank Jr. understood enough about life in the Jim Crow South to know that any job he would be able to obtain would be one of manual labor with no opportunity for advancement. Over the years he had watched Arthur, Glenda, Shirley, and Luke give their all each day at work with little to show for their efforts. He had watched Jean Ann, Dixon, and David Jackson do relatively little to no work and be rewarded with raises, cars, and new clothes. Frank Jr. decided to strike his own "fair balance" in life and make sure that life provided him with some rewards.

Arthur was able to get Frank Jr. a job on the maintenance staff at the white high school in River Wind, Mississippi, and three miles east of Waterfall. Arthur had been a valued worker on the maintenance staff at the high school for fifteen years and assured his boss, Walton Barnes, that he would make sure that Frank Jr. would more than carry his share of the workload. This promise proved to be a greater challenge for Arthur than he realized.

River Wind High School was one of the largest high schools along the Gulf Coast, with three hundred students. Along with Arthur there were four other maintenance men, two Negro and two white, with Mr. Barnes as their supervisor. Together they were responsible for the interior and exterior of the school and its property. Arthur and two other Negro men were primarily responsible for the exterior of the building and groundskeeping for all the property. There was plenty of work to be done keeping the grass cut and watered, trees and hedges trimmed, and the combination football and baseball field in mint condition. The two Negro maintenance men, Elijah Sampson and Willis Brown, were glad to hear that Mr. Barnes agreed to hire Frank Jr., as they could use all the help they could get to meet the high standards of work that Mr. Barnes expected. They often found themselves working long hours past their appointed workday to satisfy Mr. Barnes, especially when the principal of the high school had invited guests for certain events, such as the first football game each year.

Frank Jr.'s first day of work began at 6:00 a.m. on June 15, 1906. While it was not technically summer, the daytime temperature in mid-June that year was about eighty-five degrees. Arthur and the other outside maintenance men liked to start work as early as possible on the lawn and areas of the school property that had no shade from the sun. This meant working from 6:00 a.m. to 9:00 a.m., only stopping for a quick drink of water now and then. After 9:00 a.m. it would be too hot and humid to work in those open areas for more than thirty minutes at a time until after 4:00 p.m. Frank Jr. was five feet eight and 140 pounds and was able to do most of the necessary work on his first day except for the hedge trimming. There were six sets of hedges, each six feet high and in the design of a horseshoe. Arthur told Frank Jr. that he would teach him how to trim the hedges and not alter the shape of the horseshoe. Frank Jr. learned everything quickly, and after two weeks on the job he had learned the techniques of all the tasks, including hedge trimming. However, the days he enjoyed most were Fridays because every Friday was payday. Frank Jr. was earning twenty-five cents per day and was paid in cash at the end of every week. Arthur told Frank Jr. that he wanted him to save fifty cents each week, as he did not want any payment from Frank Jr. for room and board. Frank Jr. thanked Arthur for his generosity but insisted that having the ability to contribute to the family's welfare was one of the two most important reasons he wanted to work. Frank Jr. told Arthur that he would be giving him fifty cents per week for the family's living expenses, saving fifty cents, and keeping twenty-five cents for his personal spending needs. Arthur respected Frank Jr.'s decision and his desire to help support the family's needs.

The summer of 1906 went well for Frank Jr. He felt like a productive member of the family, and he enjoyed working with his uncle Arthur. The new school session started September 6, 1906. The return of the white students to the school presented new issues for Frank Jr. Arthur, Elijah Sampson, and Willis Brown tried to prepare Frank Jr. for the return of the students. They explained to him that while many of them were in his age group, they were not his friends or equals. Regardless of their ages they were all his superiors, and he must respect them as such. They told him that some of the students were nice and some ignored the staff. He had to treat them all with the same respect regardless of how they treated him. Frank Jr. understood what the men were telling him and understood that his very life could depend on following their instructions. He told them that he would do his best.

On the first day of school many of the students arrived early to greet and spend time with their friends outside on the lawn before having to go inside the building for the day. Frank Jr.'s first challenge was watching the students play games on the lawn, trampling the grass and running through the neatly trimmed horseshoe hedges, making them look as though horses had been driven through them. When the bell rang for the students to enter the school, Walton Barnes came across the lawn and told Frank Jr. to be sure to tell Arthur, Elijah, and Willis to straighten out the lawn and the hedges before they went home that day. Frank Jr. responded, "Yes, sir," but he knew that this work would take at least two to three hours to complete at the end of the day when the students were finally gone. The workday was supposed to end at 5:00 p.m. That day it ended at 7:30 p.m. When they were home, Frank Jr. asked Arthur if they would be paid extra for having to work longer hours. Almost simultaneously Arthur, Gloria, and Shirley started laughing as though Frank Jr. had told a very funny joke. When they stopped laughing, Arthur responded, "No, son, we will never get paid extra for working over our time. What we do need to be concerned about is doing good repair work after those kids leave so everything looks brand new for them the next day. Mr. Barnes expects no less from us and will hold us responsible if the work does not meet his standards no matter how much damage those kids do."

As the school year continued, Frank Jr. became more frustrated with the long workdays caused by the students. It was worse when their games included throwing each other into the hedges. When they just ran through the hedges they turned some of the branches, which had to be turned back later. However, when they threw each other on top of the hedges, they flattened and broke branches, which were difficult and sometimes impossible to repair. These situations required tying some of the remaining branches together to fill gaps and then retrimming the damaged area. It also pained Frank Jr. greatly to have to say "sir" and "ma' am" to kids his own age and younger. He felt even worse every time he heard Arthur, Elijah, and Willis using those words when talking to the kids.

Frank Jr. managed to make it through the 1906–07 school year without any problems other than mumbling loudly sometimes about what he would like to teach the kids. He had decided by Christmas that he would not work another year at the school. Frank Jr. appreciated the sacrifice Arthur, Elijah, and Willis were making for their families, and he did not want to make their workload more difficult by leaving them during the school year. The summer, when the workload was not complicated by the students, would give them time to find a replacement for him.

The school year ended on May 21, 1907. On May 22, 1907, Frank Jr. told Arthur that he would not be back the next day or any other day for work because he had had enough. Arthur actually appreciated Frank Jr.'s efforts to always stay in control of his thoughts, feelings, and words during the school year, and waiting until the school year was over before he left the job.

On the morning of May 23, 1907, around 7:00 a.m., Frank Jr. decided to take a twenty-minute walk down to the beach to sit and think for a while. As he looked out on the water, a Negro couple came and sat about thirty feet away. They seemed to be boyfriend and girlfriend enjoying some time together at the beach. About ten minutes after they arrived, Frank Jr. heard the man calling to him. Frank Jr. went over to find out what he wanted.

"Hey, boy, how would you like to make two bits (twenty-five cents)?"

"Yes, sir, I would like to make two bits. What do I have to do?"

"I want you to go over to a house on River Street, number 32, and knock on the door. When the door opens, give the person this note I just wrote and wait for them to give you a package to bring to me. Do you think you can do that?"

"Sure, mister, I can do that, and it won't take me a long time either."

"Good. Here's the note; no need for you to read it, and hurry back."

Frank Jr. knew exactly where number 32 on River Street should be and took a shortcut to save about three minutes. When he arrived at 32 River Street, Frank did as he was instructed and was given what seemed to be a bottle wrapped in a cool, wet towel. He returned to the couple as quickly as he could and gave the bundle to the man, who gave it to his girlfriend. The man was surprised to see Frank again so quickly.

"Boy, you must have wings under that shirt. That kind of effort is worth another four bits. What do you do every day to earn a living?"

"Well, sir, I quit my job yesterday, and I came to the beach this morning to think about what I would do next."

"How would you like to work for me?" Frank Jr. thought about the question and decided that since he had just earned three days' pay in a little less than twenty minutes, he could not refuse the offer.

"Sir, I would be glad to work for you. What do I have to do?"

JOE DAVID GARNER JR.

"Use your wings and run errands for me as fast as you can. If you do a good job, your pay will be one dollar per day. How does that sound to you, boy?"

"That sounds just fine to me, sir! When do I start?"

"You already have. By the way, my name is Rufus Jones. You might know me better as the Prince of Pleasure, but you can call me Mr. Jones. What's your name, boy?" Frank Jr. nodded his head, as he had indeed heard of the Prince of Pleasure, the most successful pimp on the Gulf Coast.

"Yes, sir, Mr. Jones. My name is Frank Perry Jr., Mr. Jones, and you can call me anything you want." The Prince and his girlfriend laughed out loud.

"Well, Junior, there are a few basic rules you need to know. The most important is that I am in charge, and you take orders from me and sometimes from Gloria here, my 'bottom woman,' my second in command. When I am not around, Gloria is in charge. Any questions, Junior?"

"What time do you want me to report to work each day, Mr. Jones?"

"How would you like to live in my house on River Street, Junior? That way you will never be late for work."

"I would like to, Mr. Jones, but I just need to let my aunt and uncle know because I have been living with them since my parents died when I was a baby."

"Okay, Junior. You go work things out with your aunt and uncle, and you come to my house tonight at six o'clock. That's dinner time. You will be eating with the rest of our staff in the dining area just off from the kitchen. I will let Big Jim, my bodyguard, know that you are coming. It was Big Jim that gave you the champagne."

On his walk back to his aunt Glenda and uncle Arthur's home, Frank Jr. could almost not believe how his life had changed so quickly. He not only had a new job and a new home; in twenty minutes he had earned a normal three days' pay and would now be earning more each day than his aunt Gloria, uncle Arthur, and his sister Shirley combined. Frank Jr. then thought that he had to make sure that his aunt Gloria and uncle Arthur knew how grateful he was for all they have done for him and Shirley. He would tell them that they could now count on him for at least three dollars per week instead of his old fifty cents per week, and he would not accept no for an answer. This also helped him feel better about leaving them and the only home he had known in his life.

It was more difficult than he thought it would be to tell his family that he was moving out of their home so quickly. He knew he would miss them more than they would ever know. He tried to convince himself as much as them that his new life would be better for them all because of his new job.

"Uncle Arthur, Aunt Glenda, Shirley, if it hadn't happened to me, I would not believe that something like this could happen to somebody all in one day. But everything I told you is true, and I told Mr. Jones that I would be back to his house tonight for dinner by six o'clock."

"Son, we understand and respect you for what you're doing, especially wanting to help us more, but you be real careful because Rufus Jones is a dangerous man."

"I will, Uncle Arthur. I'll be real careful."

In 1907 Rufus Jones was thirty years old, six feet two, and weighed 210 pounds. He had been a pimp for fifteen years, starting out in a partnership in 1892 with Janet and Judy Lester, twin sisters his age who lived next door. The Jones and Lester families were sharecroppers who lived and worked on the thirty-acre fruit, vegetable, and sugar cane farm of Batson Baker in River Wind. It was known and could clearly be seen by everyone that Janet and Judy's father was Batson Baker. It was Janet and Judy's caramel-colored skin that made it impossible for them to pass as white. They otherwise had a striking resemblance to Batson Baker, including green eyes and straight brown hair. When they turned fourteen, Janet and Judy's mother, Elnora, told them that she and their father, Monroe, would do the best they could to protect them from unwanted demands by men both Negro as well as white, but she wanted them to know that because they were already being noticed by grown men they might be subjected to the same treatment she received during her life, which led to their birth. She assured them that she and their father loved them dearly, always have and always would, no matter what life may bring to their doorstep.

Janet and Judy had grown up with Rufus, and they had become good friends early in life. When they became teenagers, Rufus told them that if they were ever in trouble he would help them in any way that he could. Trouble started for Janet and Judy two months before their fifteenth birthday. It came from eighteen-year-old Paul Baker, Batson Baker's son. Paul was walking across his front yard on a Sunday afternoon in September when he saw Janet and Judy walking to their cabin after attending a worship service in the cabin of Tim and Thelma Moore, two of the oldest sharecroppers on Batson Baker's farm.

"Janet! Come over here!"

"Yes, sir, Mr. Paul!"

"Follow me in the house, Janet. My folks had a party last night, and there is a lot of leftover food. I want you to take some of it for you and your family."

"Thank you, Mr. Paul. Lord knows we could use some good food."

"Over here is the room we need, Janet. Come on in."

"Mr. Paul, where we going? This room don't look like a kitchen."

"This is my bedroom, Janet. Now take off your clothes, or I will have your entire family thrown off my family's farm immediately."

"Yes, sir, Mr. Paul."

Janet had been too afraid to say no or to resist. She remembered what her mother had told her, and she told herself that her bad time had come. She was surprised that Paul would treat her this way since he knows that they are half brother and sister. When he finished with her, Paul told Janet to tell no one about what he had done. It was a week later, after waking from a nightmare, that she told her mother and Judy what had happened. The following month Paul demanded that Judy come with him to his bedroom.

Judy was always more spirited than Janet, and she told Rufus what had happened to her the very next day. She told Rufus that after Paul was done with her he said that she was not as afraid of him as Janet had been, and he gave her two dollars for not being afraid.

"If he forces you to come to his room again, tell him that you want five dollars for coming."

"I'd like to ask him, Rufus, but five dollars is a lot of money, and he might get real mad."

"If he gets mad you laugh; act surprised and say that you were just joking because you know he don't have to give you nothing."

Judy did not have to wait long before Paul called for her again the following month. She decided to give Rufus's idea a try as soon as she walked into Paul's bedroom.

"Paul, I'll give you a real good time and treat you extra nice if you give me five dollars."

"Okay, Judy, you are different. If I like it, I'll give you five dollars."

Feeling the relief of not worrying about Paul becoming angry, Judy pretended to enjoy being with him, screaming out his name and saying what a big, wonderful man he was and such.

"Well, Judy, I have to say that you were better than I expected. Here, you earned your five dollars. I'll send for you when I need you again."

When Judy told Rufus and Janet what had happened between her and Paul, they both were surprised and at the same time realized that they did not always have to be helpless victims. Rufus told them he had also learned something that was very important. It is possible to make a lot more money than two bits a day and in a lot less time.

"Janet, Judy, it's real clear that your bodies attract men who would be willing to pay to have you. Why not use what will happen to you anyway as an opportunity to make more money than you could ever make at two bits a day?"

"I can tell you that Paul didn't mind at all giving me that five dollars after I made him feel like he was a big stud horse!"

"Judy, the next time Paul calls for you, tell him that you would not mind doing the same for his friends if they would give you five dollars each time. And Janet, if you agree to do the same, I will also find Negro men for you both, but I'll only ask them for two dollars each if they are from sharecropping families."

"Rufus, that five dollars felt good in my hand, and I like the idea of thinking that if I save my money I might have enough to leave this place one day. But Janet and me would probably end up pregnant if we ain't already. And I would not do it unless Janet agrees."

"Judy, I been thinking about that kind of problem, so I had a talk with Rachael Moore, Tim and Thelma Moore's daughter. I learned from her that from age sixteen to twenty-six she had been the primary sexual interest of Batson Baker. Over that period of time Rachael had two children by Mr. Baker. I asked her how she managed not to have had more children by Mr. Baker. Rachael said that her mother taught her how to clean herself inside with a mixture of warm water and moonshine as fast as she could after being with Batson Baker. When she turned twenty-six she said that Mr. Baker lost interest in her because she started to gain weight and was too busy with her daily farm chores plus taking care of her two children she had by him."

"If y'all do this, I will be responsible for having the warm water and moonshine mix ready for you to use at anytime, in addition to finding men able to pay to be with you. My share of the money would be two dollars from every five dollars paid by each man, and fifty cents from every man who pays two dollars."

"Rufus, I'm willing to try as long as the warm water and moonshine mix keeps me from getting pregnant, and Janet agrees."

"I might as well go along because I know that Paul Baker will be calling me to his bedroom from time to time anyway, and I been watching some of the Negro men who seem to not be able to take their eyes off me when I am around them."

At the age of fifteen, Rufus, Janet, and Judy managed to work through and around all kinds of issues and problems to make their moneymaking idea pay off. Paul Baker not only agreed when Judy suggested to him that she would show his friends a good time for five dollars each, it was three months before she and Janet found out that Paul was actually charging his friends ten dollars each while giving Janet and Judy the five dollars per person he agreed to have his friends pay. Rufus continued to look for ways to do more business. He began recruiting other young attractive females on the farm, especially those who were fathered by Batson Baker, who looked more white than Negro.

In 1897, at the age of twenty, Rufus, Judy, and Janet left Batson Baker's farm and bought the ten-room house at 32 River Street for $1,000. Rufus had expanded their business to the larger community in River Wind, and they had six other girls working with them. In 1902 Rufus hired Big Jim Wells, a former prizefighter, to be his bodyguard and driver. Big Jim was six feet five and 230 pounds, but had not been a very good prizefighter. He was glad for the opportunity to work for Rufus at three dollars per day and a room in Rufus's house.

In 1897 Rufus also hired Gloria Turner. Gloria was a very attractive, dark-skinned, eighteen-year-old. She was five feet eight and weighed 115 pounds, with shoulder-length, very curly, black hair. Rufus sensed toughness in Gloria beneath her physical beauty that was uncommon for a female. Gloria approached Rufus one day as he exited his car in front of the barbershop, where he went for his weekly haircut. Gloria walked right up to him, ignoring Big Jim's words of warning to not get too close to Mr. Jones. Gloria said, "Mr. Jones,

I'm Gloria Turner, and I am here to tell you that if you let me come to work for you I will guarantee you that I will make your customers happier than they ever imagined that they could be. Everyone will know that Rufus Jones is the Prince of Pleasure, and Gloria Turner is his princess." Rufus was impressed with Gloria's confidence and her beauty. He hired her on the spot, and the men in the barbershop began referring to him as the Prince of Pleasure. Gloria not only lived up to her promise, but often served as a support to and protector of the other working girls when Rufus was not around. After six months Rufus convinced Janet and Judy to take a more business management role and let Gloria manage the girls on a day-to-day basis when he was not around. Gloria also handled all special clients personally to ensure their satisfaction. Rufus made it known to everyone that Gloria had earned the right to be his "bottom woman," the heart of his business.

When Frank Jr. began working for Rufus, he was very impressed with Rufus's intelligence and his ability to understand how to get the most productivity from his employees by finding out their strengths and weaknesses. He was also very impressed with Gloria's awareness of what the girls as well as the customers needed to make them feel good about themselves. In May 1908, after one year of working for Mr. Jones, Frank Jr. told Rufus that he had an idea that he felt would be good for the business that he would like to tell him about if he was interested. Mr. Jones said, "Sure, Junior, I'd like to hear your idea. Let's talk after dinner tonight."

That night after dinner Mr. Jones told Frank Jr. that he had about fifteen minutes before he and Gloria had to go make arrangements for a party for a special customer.

"Mr. Jones, I have seen over the last year that your best customers, those who spent the most money, were white businessmen who might be more comfortable if they did not have to come to the Negro neighborhood on River Street for their fun. Mr. Jones, I believe that if you paid for a set of rooms for one night in the expensive hotel downtown for your best-paying white customers you could make a lot of money. You could tell them that you were inviting them to a fancy party that was a civic fund-raising event to benefit orphan children. You and Gloria could select your best girls, especially those that looked more white than Negro, to be their 'dates' for the party. Some of your other girls could serve as hostesses and servers. They could pay you in the form of a specified donation for the children as a way of making a good profit on your expenses and investment."

"Junior, I'm going to give your idea some thought."

When Rufus shared Frank Jr.'s idea with Gloria, Judy, and Janet, they said they thought it would be worth a try. The four of them worked to identify the right customers and to make the hotel arrangements for one night over the July Fourth holiday weekend. Ten of their best customers were invited to the event for a donation of one hundred dollars each. The charge by the hotel was $350. Their initial profit was $650. They would have only been able to charge forty-five dollars per person at 32 River Street. Rufus gave Frank Jr. a fifty-dollar bonus at the end of the week.

Rufus continued to utilize the downtown hotel for smaller and sometimes larger parties at least once per month. Frank Jr.'s idea that white businessmen would not mind paying more money for additional comforts and to avoid spending time in the Negro neighborhood increased their annual incomes threefold. In October 1897, Rufus raised Frank Jr.'s daily pay to ten dollars per day.

Frank Jr. was able to give his aunt Glenda, uncle Arthur, and sister Shirley thirty dollars per week instead of the three dollars he had promised. They still had concerns about Frank Jr.'s safety but were grateful for his generous financial help, which enabled Glenda and Arthur to retire at age sixty while they were still in good health. Frank Jr. worked for Rufus until 1922, when he turned thirty years old. He had managed his money wisely and bought himself a three-bedroom home in Waterfall and a 1922 Ford. To the joy of his aunt Glenda, uncle Arthur, and sister Shirley, Frank Jr. joined them as a member of Beulah Baptist Church in Waterfall. The day he was baptized, Shirley told him that she was sure that their parents were happy and proud of them both, especially their commitment to God and family.

CHAPTER 4

THE WILLIE MORGAN STORY

On May 18, 1967, after my father closed his barbershop for the day he came into the house and told my mother and me the story of Willie Morgan's dog with no fleas.

It was such a hot day, at 4:30 p.m. all the regulars had gone for the day, and he was finishing with his last customer, Dennis Brown, the best Negro electrician within thirty miles. Dennis was about forty-seven years old, six feet tall, and weighed 185 pounds. He had little formal education. He learned his electrical skills by working as a helper for Wilford Branch, a white professional electrician, from the time he was fourteen years old. It was said that Dennis could solve any electrical problem in a house, and since he was not a licensed electrician his prices were very affordable. Dennis had a reputation for doing good work, being on time, and completing the work on his stated completion schedule. While Dennis was still in the barber chair, Willie Morgan arrived. Willie was about fifty years old, five feet eight, weighed 170 pounds, and was officially retired with a military disability. However, he was as strong as any man in the county and often worked as a house painter. Willie was also an alcoholic and would drink just about anything that contained alcohol.

When Willie arrived at the barbershop, it was obvious that he had been drinking for some time. Before anyone could respond to his initial greeting, he began talking nonstop about how his dog was the best rabbit hunting dog in the world, and what made the dog even more special was that it had no fleas. My father and Dennis started laughing loudly. Willie took offense at their laughter.

"I'll take any bet and prove that my dog can find more rabbits than any other dog in the county in a day of hunting."

Dennis responded, "Willie, you might well have the best hunting dog in the county, but we were laughing because you said the dog had no fleas."

"Well, Dennis Brown, you willing to put your money where your mouth is?"

"Willie, you're drunk. Go home and go to bed."

"Yeah, I'm drunk, but you got no guts, Dennis Brown. You're afraid to put your money where your mouth is."

"Willie, your dog does hunt—in the woods. He lives in your yard. The woods and your yard, my yard, everybody's yard is full of fleas. It would be impossible for your dog not to have fleas."

"Bet then, Dennis Brown, you so sure my dog has fleas. Bet! Bet! I bet you one hundred dollars. Now, put up or shut up, Dennis Brown."

"Willie, I don't need or want your money. How would you go about proving such a thing anyway?"

"I will go get my dog now and let y'all check him for fleas. If you don't find any, you give me one hundred dollars."

"Willie, if I wanted to bet, first of all, you don't have one hundred dollars, and second, you don't even know where your dog is right now."

"I know where my dog is, and I will bring him here in thirty minutes."

"Willie, my haircut is done now, and I am going home, and I am tired of your drunken foolishness."

"You are a coward, Dennis Brown! That is why you are going home. So go home, coward!"

"Okay, Willie, I'm going to take your bet. Where is your one hundred dollars? Here is mine."

"I will bring my one hundred dollars when I come back with my dog, even though I know I don't need it."

"Willie, be back with the dog in thirty minutes and don't have me to come look for you."

"I'll be back in thirty minutes, Dennis Brown; just make sure you don't leave."

After one hour Willie had not returned. Dennis had calmed down and said he would wait another fifteen minutes and then go home. He said that he was no longer mad at Willie because he knew Willie was crazy drunk from drinking wood alcohol, which Willie sometimes made himself from ingredients he fermented in his bathtub. As Dennis was getting his hat to go home, Willie returned with his dog.

"Now, Dennis Brown, find a flea on my dog."

My father and Dennis started laughing when they took a closer look at the dog. The dog was completely wet and soap was visible on parts of his body.

Dennis said, "Willie, you have been at home all this time washing your dog! I'm not going to bother with this wet dog! Here, take this ten dollars and go buy some good moonshine at Ms. Holly's house and stop drinking that homemade wood alcohol. That stuff will kill you."

Willie took the ten dollars and continued talking nonstop about his dog being the best rabbit hunting dog in the county, and he had no fleas, as he walked in the direction of Ms. Holly's house.

CHAPTER 5

THE WARD ELLIS STORY

Amos "Deacon" Bailey was also a World War II veteran. Deacon was fifty years old and worked as a mechanic at the Hi Pep service station on Old Cross Road. He was proud of his status as deacon at Third Baptist Church, and he enjoyed coming to the barbershop on Saturdays to be with the other men to listen to and tell stories. Deacon would usually greet the men by saying something like, "I knew I'd find y'all here hiding from your wives. Go ahead; tell the truth, y'all scared of them women, ain't you?" Someone would respond with, "No more than you're scared of yours!" During the war Deacon was a corporal stationed at Camp Dawson in Crest Ridge, Mississippi, assigned to the motor pool. Deacon worked alongside Staff Sergeant Vern Culver, one of the smartest mechanics he had ever met until a kid named Ward Ellis came along. One of the stories Deacon enjoyed telling most was about Ward Ellis.

From 1945 to 1970, Ward Ellis was considered the best engine mechanic in a six-county area of southeast Mississippi. He joined the army in July 1940 at the age of twenty and was assigned to the motor pool. Ward would later say that the army motor pool gave him a second new lease on life.

Ward was born in his parents' home in Flatwheel, Mississippi, on July 3, 1920. Flatwheel was a small town with a post office, a bank, and a curb store. Flatwheel's 120 citizens conducted their important business affairs in Crest Ridge, a city of about thirty thousand in 1940, about three miles north of Flatwheel. Ward's parents, Albert and Gladys Ellis, both born in 1900, had no formal education but had worked hard since their marriage in 1915 toward the goal of one day owning their own home. Before their marriage they would talk for hours about the pride and joy they would feel the day they would make their final payment on their home. They also hoped that it would be their family's home for generations to come. They agreed that they would have a better chance of achieving their goal if they waited to get married until after they both found work other than sharecropping. In July 1915, Albert was hired as a laborer in Gillman's Farm Supplies store in Crest Ridge. At the age of fifteen, Albert was five feet eleven and weighed 185 pounds and able to handle the heavy lifting required in Mr. Gillman's store. Gladys was five feet six and weighed 120 pounds and was hired by Stevens' Dry Cleaners, also in Crest Ridge, to clean, sew, and iron special garments such as police and fire department uniforms and delicate fabrics. Albert and Gladys were married in September 1915. To save money, Albert and Gladys continued to live with their parents for one year. In October 1916, Albert managed to convince Mr. Thomas Gillman, owner of Gillman's Farm Supplies, to allow him and Gladys to rent a two-bedroom cabin in Flatwheel that was owned by Mr. Gillman. Albert told Mr. Gillman that if he was pleased with his work for one year, he would like to talk with him again about a plan to buy the cabin. Mr. Gillman was impressed with young Albert's focus, determination, and seeming appreciation for the value of hard work, and he agreed to Albert's request. In October 1917, Albert and Mr. Gillman agreed on a payment plan for the purchase of the cabin.

Ward's birth was the happiest day Albert and Gladys had shared since their wedding. They were committed to working even harder to make sure they were able to pay Mr. Gillman the balance due on the cabin and to give their son the best opportunity for success in life. They agreed that one of the most important things they had to provide for Ward was the opportunity for an education and to obtain a high school diploma. No sacrifice on their part would be too great to achieve this goal. They knew that a high school diploma would mean the difference between a life of unending struggle and a life that could be rewarding and provide a principal building block for the family for generations to come.

Albert and Gladys were convinced that at the age of six months Ward enjoyed listening to music and song. Gladys had a nice alto singing voice and loved to sing. Whenever Ward heard her sing, he would give his full attention to her. Ward's first attempt to speak was trying to sing along with Gladys when he was eighteen months old. Gladys's mother, Martha, also loved to sing and sang to Ward whenever she cared for him while Gladys was working. Occasionally Gladys had to take Ward with her to work on days her mother had to travel into Crest Ridge to wash and iron for Clayton Wyles, the owner of the Ford car dealership. Orvil Stevens and his wife, Victoria, the owners of Stevens' Dry Cleaners, had given their consent for Gladys to bring Ward with her when necessary, as Ward never caused Gladys to get behind in her work. Mr. and Mrs. Stevens had a twenty-two-year-old daughter, Virginia, who also worked in the dry cleaners and enjoyed having Ward come to visit. Virginia usually spent more time attending to Ward than Gladys. She was an only child and was accustomed to having things her own way. Her parents had also been particularly protective of her because of her relatively small size. Virginia was five feet three and weighed 110 pounds. She dressed conservatively, usually wearing high neckline dresses that covered her ankles. However, since her junior year in college, she loved wearing makeup that made her face appear darker and wore her shoulder-length, black hair unbound. Her mother worried that Virginia was being influenced by "the wrong crowd," as she called them.

When Ward was eight months old, Gladys noticed that Virginia had started reading to Ward from various books. Gladys never wanted to acknowledge her awareness of this because she did not want anyone to know how much she valued Ward being introduced to books and hopefully developing a desire to read. Gladys made sure she brought Ward to the dry cleaners as often as possible without appearing to have any interest in Virginia reading to Ward. The books Virginia read to Ward were the same children's books her parents bought and read to her as a child.

When Ward started to speak around age two, Virginia started teaching him the names of objects and people around him. When he turned three, he told Virginia that he wanted to read the books himself. Virginia laughed and said, "Well, Ward

Ellis, I guess I'll have to teach you to read!" While growing increasingly grateful, Gladys continued to pretend to not be interested in Virginia's efforts to teach Ward to read. She and Albert hoped that Virginia would never tire of teaching Ward to read, as her books were far more advanced than the books being utilized at any level in the colored school that Ward would have to attend when he turned six years old. Virginia had completed college at Orion State University in Plum Hill, Mississippi and was capable of providing Ward with a much better education than he could receive in the colored school.

When Virginia completed college, she told her parents that since the dry cleaners business was financially very successful, she would delay indefinitely looking for a job in her major of English. Virginia's work assignment in the dry cleaners was to relieve and work with her mother whenever necessary at the front desk. Virginia found the task of greeting customers and listening to their dry cleaning needs boring and often spent her time reading. When Gladys asked if she could bring Ward to the dry cleaners when necessary, Mr. and Mrs. Stevens were concerned because they thought Gladys would be distracted and unable to do her usual good work. However, they thought Gladys might be more distracted if they refused her request, and she would then spend most of the workday worried about Ward. When Virginia showed interest in spending time with Ward, her parents were relieved because Gladys was able to keep all her attention on work, and Virginia's contribution to the work of the dry cleaners was for the most part nonexistent. Mr. and Mrs. Stevens were also glad to see their daughter doing something positive that she seemed to enjoy.

Virginia continued her interest in Ward, and when he turned seven she gave him a small desktop toy piano. Virginia was impressed with Ward's ability to remember her instructions about the keys on the piano. Ward could also at age seven read Virginia's fourth-grade history book with ease. On Ward's ninth birthday, Virginia suggested that Ward help out at the dry cleaners as often as possible after school sweeping and mopping the floor, cleaning the bathroom, and keeping the sidewalk in front of the store clean. Virginia said she would give Ward ten cents per week from her own money. Her parents and Ward's parents agreed. When Ward reached age eleven, he had already excelled far beyond the books and resources of the colored school and had lost interest in continuing to attend. He told his parents that he would rather go to the dry cleaners every day and be taught by Virginia. Gladys and Albert explained to Ward that they knew he would not learn much more at the colored school, but they did not want to take the chance that Mr. and Mrs. Stevens would see such a request as an imposition and possibly forbid him from returning to the dry cleaners at all. Ward was disappointed, but understood his parents' concern and fear. However, Ward believed that he had a good relationship with Virginia and decided to tell her about his idea. Virginia agreed and presented the idea to her parents. Mr. and Mrs. Stevens reluctantly gave their permission. When Virginia told Ward about her parents' consent, he could not wait to tell his parents.

To Gladys's and Albert's surprise, all went well until 1932, when Ward was twelve years old. Since Virginia's graduation from college and her reluctance to seek employment, her parents hoped that she would get married. Virginia had dated several young men but none seriously until she met

Roger Dell. Roger was thirty-four years old, five feet nine, weighed 175 pounds, and worked as an associate lawyer in his father's law practice in Crest Ridge. He and Virginia began dating on an occasional basis in 1930. In 1932 they began dating regularly and decided to become engaged in September 1932. Virginia's mother was particularly happy about this, as she commented often to Virginia that with Roger's blue eyes and blond hair, they would have beautiful children. With urging from their parents, their mothers in particular, they decided to get married on June 1, 1933. With financial support from their parents, Roger and Virginia purchased a three-bedroom home in the suburbs of Crest Ridge. Virginia's mother told her that it was no longer necessary for her to return to the dry cleaners, as she should now become a homemaker and hopefully a mother very soon. With Virginia's departure from the dry cleaners, Ward's ability to enhance his academic education ended as well as his ten cents per week job. As it was very clear that there would be no point in Ward returning to the colored school, Albert and Gladys told Ward that he would need to get work on one of the farms near Flatwheel, as he was too young and physically small to get a manual labor job in Crest Ridge. At age twelve, Ward was about five feet tall and weighed about 105 pounds.

Phillip Duncan owned a two hundred-acre farm that began about a quarter mile from the Ellis home. Mr. Duncan was considered a fair man by the colored men and women that worked on his farm, and he was always willing to take on more workers provided they worked hard enough for him to increase the sales of his farm products. Albert and Gladys decided that they would ask their neighbor, George Jackson, if Ward could accompany his sixteen-year-old son, William, to Mr. Duncan's farm to seek employment. William had been working for Mr. Duncan since he was twelve years old and was considered a very good worker by Mr. Duncan. Mr. Jackson agreed and said that William would come by to get Ward the next morning at 5:15 a.m.

Ward was not looking forward to working on Mr. Duncan's farm, but he understood that it was necessary, as there were no other good options available. The next morning Gladys made sure that Ward had a good breakfast and was ready by 5:00 a.m. She also prepared a ham sandwich and an apple for his lunch. Albert told Ward that if Mr. Duncan agreed to give him a chance to work, he needed to give his very best effort to do whatever he was asked, if for no other reason than that the other farm owners were not as fair and had little to no regard for their colored workers. Ward told him that he would do his best.

William Jackson knocked on the Ellis's front door promptly at 5:15 a.m. Ward and Albert came right out to greet him. Albert thanked William for agreeing to help Ward get a job on Mr. Duncan's farm. William said he was glad to help and if Mr. Duncan gives Ward a job, he would come by every morning to take Ward to the farm with him and bring him back home at the end of the day. William and Ward were not friends but knew each other from their brief time together at the colored school. Their families were also good neighbors, and they all attended Beulah Street Baptist Church.

"Ward, when we get there I will do all the talking to Mr. Duncan. If he speaks to you, you be sure to say 'yes, sir' and 'no, sir.'"

"Okay, William."

"Mr. Duncan is generally a good man, but he will only hire colored people who he thinks know that they need to respect him. Mr. Duncan believes that respect for him shows a willingness to work hard. In my four years of working for Mr. Duncan, I never saw him do harm or allow harm to any of his colored workers."

William was five feet eight and weighed 160 pounds. He was basically the same height and weight as Mr. Duncan. When William and Ward arrived at Mr. Duncan's farm, Mr. Duncan was explaining to Sidney Green, one of his most trusted colored workers, that he needed to go to Crest Ridge to buy two new plows. The weather had been near perfect for the last two years, and Mr. Duncan had decided to use five extra acres of his farm to grow additional vegetables— primarily tomatoes, cucumbers, lettuce, corn, field peas, and butter beans—for the local and out-of-state market. Mr. Duncan asked Sidney to select two mules and a crew of six men to start preparing the additional five acres for planting. William waited for Mr. Duncan to finish his instructions to Sidney before introducing Ward. Before William finished his introduction, Mr. Duncan knew that he would ask him to consider hiring Ward. Given his plan to expand the farm work to five more acres, Mr. Duncan was already thinking about adding a few more workers. He waited patiently for William to finish his introduction of Ward and his request on Ward's behalf for employment. Mr. Duncan was impressed with William's understanding that Ward was small in stature and would need help learning how to manage the work.

"Mr. Duncan, if you decide to hire Ward, I promise to be responsible for showing him what has to be done and making sure that he does it like you want it done."

"All right, William. I'm going to give Ward here a try with your guarantee that he will be a good worker for me. He starts work right now, and I will make a final decision about hiring him in about a week."

"Thank you, Mr. Duncan."

"I thank you too, Mr. Duncan, sir. I promise to work hard for you just like William."

Ward was glad for the opportunity to work, primarily to help his family, not because he had any desire to learn farm work or to become a farmer. He wasn't sure what he wanted to do to earn a living, but he knew he wanted to utilize his brain and not his back.

William knew that he needed to give Ward on-the-job training, as Sidney and the six men he selected would begin the work of clearing the five additional acres that day, and new work assignments would be made by the next day. William took Ward to the barn, where fifteen cows for milking were kept.

"Ward, have you ever milked a cow before?"

"No."

"It's easy. Watch me; I'm going to show you how it's done. You're going to be helping Calvin Davis, Mitchell Anderson, and Larry Harrison, three longtime sharecroppers for Mr. Duncan, milk the cows each morning when you arrive. After you finish milking the cows, you will go over to the horse barn with Calvin, Mitchell, and Larry to feed and groom ten riding horses. These horses are used by Mr. Duncan, his family, and guests. They needed to be ready for riding whenever Mr. Duncan needs them. One of the benefits of taking care of the riding horses is that they need to be exercised on a regular basis. Mr. Duncan gave Calvin, Mitchell, and Larry permission to ride the horses to keep them in good condition. They will teach you to ride."

"Taking care of the cows and horses will keep you busy most days; however, you might have to work on any task anytime as necessary. This usually happens when Mr. Duncan receives a special order from one of his buyers, or if he adds on more work like clearing an additional five acres for planting. After a few years you will have learned every job on the farm."

For the next eight years Ward worked on Mr. Duncan's farm. As William had told him, he learned to do every job on the farm. Ward's understanding that he was needed to help his family financially continued to be the driving force that kept him coming back to Mr. Duncan's farm each day. He also grew fond of Mr. Duncan's riding horses. Calvin, Mitchell, and Larry were still very capable riders well into their fifties, but they began to give more and more of the exercise riding duties to Ward and Anthony Jefferson, who came to work on the farm as a fourteen-year-old when Ward was eighteen. Ward liked Anthony because Anthony was an eager learner. One day in the stable, Anthony saw Ward reading a book unlike any he had seen in the colored school.

"What kind of book you reading, Ward?"

"It's a history book all about ancient Rome that a friend of mine gave me."

"You look like you having fun reading. Can you teach me how to read a book like that, Ward?"

"Sure, Anthony, I'll be glad to."

Ward felt a sense of pride and self-worth being able to teach Anthony better reading skills. Anthony's fast learning and constant expressions of appreciation were also very satisfying. But most importantly, what Ward could see in Anthony's eyes that was not there before, was hope. Ward realized that hope makes life worth living, instead of just surviving. Ward knew that what he saw in the eyes of William, Sidney, Calvin, Mitchell, Larry, and the other workers was survival ability in the here and now. What he saw in Anthony's eyes was the future based on hope. He knew then that he could never let that same hope within him—that had developed so strongly when Virginia taught him to read—begin to dim. Ward told Anthony about the world beyond what his eyes could see.

Ward's most prized possessions were the books given to him by Virginia. On May 6, 1920, Anthony's sixteenth birthday, Ward gave him a book about the history of Mississippi.

"Anthony, this book will help you understand the past and the present and help you build a better future for yourself."

Ward could see how much Anthony appreciated this special gift, and he believed that Anthony would give his best effort to continue to learn and build on his inner hope for the future. Ward hoped and prayed that Anthony's future would not be bound by the boundaries of Mr. Duncan's farm.

On his twentieth birthday, just two months after Anthony's sixteenth, Ward knew it was time that he did something about his own future, which he definitely did not want bound by the boundaries of Mr. Duncan's farm or the state of Mississippi. On a Saturday afternoon in September in Crest Ridge during the city's Founders' Day celebration, Ward noticed soldiers in their uniforms who were home on leave. While most were white men, he saw a few colored soldiers in army uniforms. Ward was impressed at a distance with the way they walked. They seemed to have confidence and purpose. These two qualities were missing for most of the colored men he knew. He caught up with two of the colored soldiers and introduced himself and asked them what life was like for them in the army. The soldiers told Ward if he could tell them where they could get a good meal they would tell him all about the army. Ward took them to the west side of town, where most of the Negroes shopped. He told them that there were three colored-owned restaurants on the west side that had good food but that the best was Mama's Kitchen.

When they arrived at Mama's Kitchen, Ward led them to a booth in the back, away from most of the noise. A waitress came over right away to take their orders. After placing their orders the soldiers introduced themselves and began telling Ward about their lives in the army.

"My name is Raymond Coleman. I'm nineteen years old, and I'm from Franklin Oaks, Georgia. I left home at the age of seventeen to join the army. At five feet ten and 180 pounds, no one questioned me when I said I was eighteen. My mother, Flora, was forty-five years old when I joined the army and was a domestic worker. She spent a lot of time away from home working in the homes of city officials in Franklin Oaks. My father, Thomas, had been a day laborer and was sometimes away from home for days and weeks depending on the time of the year and what crops were being planted or harvested or if a construction job was available. My father was fifty years old at his death when I joined the army. Me and my three younger brothers—Otis, age, thirteen, George, age eleven, and Michael, age nine—were primarily cared for by our sixty-three-year-old maternal grandmother, Ruth, and our older sister, Barbara, age twenty-one. Barbara was taught to be a homemaker by my mother and grandmother. Barbara never had the opportunity to attend school, as my grandma's early onset arthritis progressed at a fast pace, and my mother needed as much help caring for her as she did with me and my younger brothers."

"My mother, grandmother, and sister did their best to care for me and my brothers. Mine and my family's problem had been with my father. He would usually spend most of the money he made before he came home, so he had relatively little to give to my mother for all the time he spent away. What made matters unbearable was that he was drunk and physically abusive 95 percent of the time he was home. My mother and grandmother tried to bear most of the abuse and keep him away from me, Barbara, and my younger brothers. However, the older he became the worse his abuse became toward everyone in the family. On my seventeenth birthday I realized that as the next oldest male in the family it was time for me to take matters in my own hands and stop my father from abusing us."

"My father was six feet two and weighed 210 pounds. When he returned home after a week of working on a short-term construction job just over the state line in South Carolina, I walked down the road to meet him."

"I came out here to tell you that your drunkenness and abuse ain't going to be tolerated no more in our house."

"Boy, who told you to say that to me?"

"Nobody told me to say it, and I mean every word."

"Boy, you ain't man enough yet to throw me out of my own house."

"I was as prepared as I could be for this showdown with my father, and I wanted it to end one way or another right there on the road to our house before my mother, grandmother, or Barbara could try to get involved. Before he came home I had found six full whisky bottles he had left in the house and put them in a sack. I had also hidden an identical sack in the brush with a water moccasin—a poisonous snake—inside.

"When my father brushed me aside and continued walking toward our house, I yelled to him. When he turned around I started taking the whisky bottles out of the sack that I had with me and threw them on the rocks on the side of the road. After the second bottle my father realized that I was breaking his whisky bottles."

"He started running toward me yelling, 'Boy, that's my whiskey that I paid good money that you breaking! If you don't stop, I will kill you!'"

"I turned and started running and continued to break all the bottles except one, which I had in my back pocket. My father continued to chase me as he swore he would kill me as soon as he caught me. I knew he would kill me in a fight, but I also knew I could run faster than he could. I ran into the large brush where I had the second sack hidden and made the switch before my father could see me. My other big advantage over my father was that I was a very good swimmer, and he could not swim at all. The white landowner near our home had dug a large lake and stocked it with fish for his personal use. The lake was shallow on one end and about twelve to fourteen feet deep in the middle and far end. I believed that I would have just enough time to make it to the far end of the lake before my father could catch me. When I reached the far end of the lake I made sure that he could see me drop the last bottle in the sack. When my father got about thirty feet away I laid the sack down, turned, and jumped into the deep end of the lake. He stopped at the edge and cursed at me and swore again that he would kill me. He continued to glare at me while he reached into the sack to get the whisky bottle and was bitten twice by the moccasin before he could get his hand out."

"My father was not sure what had bitten him until he saw the moccasin slink out of the bag. He knew he needed help right away and ran for our house, as he had no anticipation of being helped by the white landowner of the lake. I swam out of the lake and followed him at a safe distance. When he was close to the house he started shouting for help. My mother and grandmother came out into the yard."

"That worthless boy tricked me into getting bit by a water moccasin. I need help to get some of the poison out of my hand so I can get to a doctor. I swear I'm gonna kill that boy when I get back from the doctor."

"Lie down on the picnic table, Thomas, while Flora and me get some things from the house to get the poison out of your hand."

"Until he swore to kill me, my mother and grandmother were considering helping him. They went into the house, locked and bolted the front door, then took Barbara and my brothers out the back door and went into the woods. My father passed out in a few minutes and died later on the picnic table."

"After I was sure he was dead I got a rope and our mule and dragged his body down to the pigpen, where I buried him in an eight-foot hole in the middle of the pen. The next day I went into town and joined the army, and I have never regretted that decision or the action I took against my father. The army is now my home, and I want to stay in the army for as long as possible. The army has and continues to provide me with the best means possible to help my family. I only need a little money in the army, as all my basic needs are provided to me free. I have kept my promise to my mother to send her the majority of my army paycheck to make sure that my three younger brothers get the best education possible so that their futures will never be limited to becoming sharecroppers. Two months ago I was promoted to corporal, and one day I hope to become a master sergeant."

Then the other soldier spoke.

"My name is Charles Clifford. I am twenty-six years old, and I am from Cold Rock, Florida. I joined the army at the age of twenty, and last March I was made a staff sergeant. Like Raymond, I hope to be a master sergeant one day. I worked on various farms since the age of fourteen and was harshly treated on most of them. I decided at the age of twenty that I had to make a better life for myself somehow. One day while walking by the train station in Cold Rock, I saw a white soldier struggling with his bags to get to the train. I went over to the soldier and asked him if he would like some help carrying his bags to the train. After getting his bags on the train, the soldier gave me a dollar. I was amazed at getting a dollar for a few minutes work and at that moment, with very little knowledge of the army, decided to join. I never forgot that soldier or the emblem on his hat. I later understood that the soldier held the rank of major."

Ward thanked Raymond and Charles for telling him about the army and how it had changed their lives for the better. He also appreciated their honesty when they said that the army was not always fair to colored soldiers, but they never regretted their decisions to join, especially since it had provided a way for them to help support their families. When he left Mama's Kitchen, Ward went home to tell his parents that he would be joining the army the next day.

Albert and Gladys were not really shocked by Ward's decision to join the army, as they both expected something different from him at some point in his life. They never believed that Ward would become a sharecropper for life. While they had concerns and would always worry about his safety, they knew that Ward would have to follow his own mind.

Ward joined the army in July 1940, and was assigned to Camp Dawson in Crest Ridge for his basic training. He was in good physical condition, so basic training did not present any physical obstacles that he could not overcome. Ward spent most of his free time learning as much as possible about how the army works. He would go to the library to read about army and military history and talk to any experienced soldiers who would take the time to talk to him about their knowledge and experiences in the army.

On a Saturday morning while waiting in line to enter the mess hall for breakfast, he was told by one of the camp's staff sergeants that he had "volunteered" to clean one of the captain's jeeps and take it to the officers' living quarters. Ward reported to the motor pool and said that he had come to clean the captain's jeep. He was told by one of the motor pool mechanics, Staff Sergeant Vern Culver that something was wrong with the captain's jeep, and it had to be repaired first. Ward asked if he could watch while the repairs were being done. Sergeant Culver gave permission for him to watch. Ward not only watched but constantly asked questions about the repair work. Sergeant Culver told him that if he was going to ask questions he had to help do the work. Ward was more than glad to help. Right away Ward began to learn about the mechanic's tools and how they are used. Sergeant Culver was impressed with how fast Ward learned and retained information. No matter how many tools he told

Ward about, Ward could retrieve any tool again by name or purpose. When Sergeant Culver finished repairing the captain's jeep, he told Ward to come by again if he wanted to learn more about the motor pool. Ward was very glad to hear this invitation and returned to the motor pool at every opportunity in his schedule.

After two weeks and every spare hour he could find to work with Sergeant Culver in the motor pool, Sergeant Culver made a formal request to have Ward assigned on a permanent basis to the motor pool. In his request he stated that in his five years of work in the motor pool and his five years of working in his father's service station and car repair shop prior to joining the army, he had never seen anyone learn road vehicle and motor repair as quickly and effectively as Ward. Sergeant Culver said that he was also very impressed with Ward's dedication, dependability, and personal pride in doing quality work. When Lieutenant Morton Gates received Sergeant Culver's request, he was very intrigued, as Sergeant Culver not only had never made such a request before but had never commented on the work of any mechanic in the motor pool. Lieutenant Gates called Sergeant Culver into his office to further discuss his unusual request. In five minutes of listening to Sergeant Culver describe Ward, his abilities, and the supervised work he had allowed Ward to do in the motor pool, Lieutenant Gates felt that he would be doing Sergeant Culver and the army a grave disservice if he did not approve Sergeant Culver's request. Lieutenant Gates told Sergeant Culver that he would make his best effort to have the request approved.

In one week Lieutenant Gates informed Sergeant Culver that his very unusual request had been approved. When Ward

Ellis completed his six weeks of basic training he would be assigned to the motor pool at Camp Dawson as his first assignment. When Sergeant Culver gave the news to Ward, Ward told him that he did not know how to thank him for his effort on his behalf, but assured him that he would give his best effort every day to do the best work possible. Sergeant Culver told him that if he did not feel certain about that already he would never have made the request.

For the next five years Ward learned to become an expert mechanic with the skill to work on any vehicle that could travel on a road surface. Sergeant Culver made sure that when Ward was honorably discharged in November 1945, he also received a certificate as a licensed certified mechanic. He and Lieutenant Gates also provided Ward with a complete set of mechanic's tools sufficient to start his own repair shop, which is exactly what Ward did when he returned to Flatwheel. Initially, he started his repair shop in Flatwheel. With the help of his friends from Phillip Duncan's farm, William Jackson, Sidney Green, Calvin Davis, Mitchell Anderson, and Larry Harrison, he built a very efficient small garage next to his parents' house. Word quickly spread, primarily by his friends, that an expert mechanic was available in Flatwheel at very reasonable prices. Ward's first big break came when he made a visit to the home of Virginia and Roger Dell.

"Well, Ward Ellis, you are a sight for sore eyes. I am so glad to know that things went so well for you in the army, and you are about to start your own business!"

"Well, Miss Virginia, I owe much of it to you and all the time you took teaching me to read."

"Ward, I have to tell you that teaching you to read was the only good thing I ever did or cared about at the dry cleaners, and I can't wait to come to your car repair shop. As a matter of fact, I will be there tomorrow!"

True to her word, Virginia arrived the next day at 11:00 a.m. driving her 1940 Buick, and her husband, Roger, was driving his 1939 Ford.

"Now, Ward, from this day forward it will be up to you to be sure that our cars are in the best condition possible. And you be on the lookout for my parents and Roger's parents to be bringing their cars to you as well. I made it clear to them that no other mechanic in Mississippi is to touch any of our cars."

The quality of Ward's work became an easy message for the Stevens and the Dells to share with their friends. Phillip Duncan also heard about Ward's repair shop from all of his best farm workers. After Ward's work to repair the motor of a $3,000 tractor that he thought was no longer repairable, Mr. Duncan told Ward that he would pay him to come to his farm on a regular basis to do maintenance for all of his farm equipment.

In June of 1950, Ward opened his first auto repair shop on the west side of Crest Ridge. By 1955, he had become one of the most successful auto mechanics and businessmen in Crest Ridge, employing a total of fifteen people in both of his shops, six in Flatwheel and nine in Crest Ridge. In 1955, he built a three-bedroom home for his parents and siblings in Flatwheel. Ward also had hopes of building a three-bedroom home for himself and Doris Jackson, William's younger sister, who he had been dating seriously for the previous three years.

In 1970, after providing for the basic financial security of his family, Ward sold 70 percent of his auto repair business, which included six shops across South Mississippi, and only worked in a supervisory capacity. He continued to make a sufficient income and enjoy time with his wife, Doris, and their three children, Ward Jr., Vern, and Virginia. Some of Ward's most enjoyable moments were spent telling his children about his life, especially how his life was changed by Virginia Stevens and Sergeant Vern Culver.

CHAPTER 6

THE DELMER BLACKMON STORY

Delmer Blackmon was a kindhearted seventy-year-old gentleman about five feet seven and weighing about 150 pounds. He was one of the few men that my father never charged for his haircut. Unfortunately, he was best known for his many years of being an alcoholic and unemployable. However, my father's older cousin, Rudy Garner, also seventy years old, grew up with Delmer, and on Saturday afternoon, August 13, 1965, told the following story about Delmer, his life, his daughter, Carmen, and grandson, Kendall Kramer Jr., for everyone who was not present in the shop on April 3, 1965, when Delmer brought his letter from his daughter.

From the time Delmer was able to work in his early teens, he performed farm and any kind of day labor he could find. This continued until he was about forty-five years of age. During these working years he was known as being physically strong and able to defend himself, even though he did not have a large frame. In 1935, when Delmer was forty years old, he was a regular drinking customer at Ms. Holly's house on Friday nights. Women also frequented Ms.

Holly's house for various reasons. One group of women in particular found Ms. Holly's house to be one of the few places they could feel comfortable because Ms. Holly made sure they felt welcome because of what they shared in common. These women were the product of Negro mothers and white men. Some of them attempted to live as though they were white women. This was not possible for others because it was clear that they had Negro and white features, which made it difficult for them to be accepted by Negroes or whites. Erma Griffin was a little too dark skinned to pass as white. However, the shape of her facial features and the texture of her hair were very much Caucasian. Erma was five feet five and weighed 110 pounds.

One Friday night at Ms. Holly's house, Delmer offered to buy Erma Griffin a drink. He decided to order some of Ms. Holly's best moonshine. Erma was glad to receive his offer of Ms. Holly's best moonshine and to have someone to talk to who did not seem to judge her. They enjoyed their drinks and conversation. One drink led to another, and Delmer invited Erma to spend the night with him at Ms. Holly's house. She accepted. The next morning they agreed that they both had had an enjoyable evening and night, but they would not plan to get together again because Erma was awaiting word from her sister in Chicago about coming to live with her.

Erma moved to Chicago one week later. Nine months later, Erma gave birth to Carmen. It was clearly Delmer's baby, as she had not dated anyone since arriving in Chicago. Erma named her baby Carmen Griffin. She wrote a letter to Delmer telling him about Carmen, but making it clear that she did not expect him to come to Chicago or help in any way to care for the baby. Delmer responded by immediately sending Erma fifty dollars, which was half of all the money he had, and a promise to continue to do what he could to help care for Carmen. Delmer also asked if he could come and see the baby. Erma wrote back and told him how much she appreciated the fifty dollars, and that she would like for him to see Carmen one day when it was less likely for questions to be raised about Carmen's father. Erma said that thus far Carmen appeared to be a white baby, and there may be a possibility that she could tell people she was working as a nanny for a white family that allowed her to bring the child home from time to time because they did not want her in their home when they were out of town. Delmer wrote Erma back and said that he would respect her wishes for Carmen, as he also wanted her to have the best life possible.

As the years went by, Delmer sent whatever he could to Erma for Carmen and hoped that one day he would get to see them both. Erma wrote to him often and sent pictures of Carmen. Carmen indeed looked completely white, with no obvious Negro features.

When Delmer turned forty-five and still had not been allowed to see Carmen, who was now five years old, he began drinking more. The more he drank the less he worked, and the less he had to send to Erma for Carmen.

In 1945, when Delmer turned fifty, he lost all hope of ever being allowed to see Carmen. He stopped working on a regular basis and started to spend most of his money drinking, and he also stopped writing to Erma.

On Friday, April 2, 1965, Delmer received a letter from Carmen, now thirty years old, which he could not believe was real. He thought the letter must be from someone else, and he was just too drunk to see clearly. Delmer brought the letter to the barbershop and asked one of the men to read it for him. Bobby Graham, an eighteen-year-old, was closest to Delmer, and Delmer handed the letter to him.

Bobby opened the envelope and immediately said, "It's a short letter."

"Dear Father, I hope this letter finds you alive and well. I have thought of you often over my life and made a promise to myself that one day I would reach out to you and hopefully meet you face to face. I have so much I want to say to you. All I want to say in this letter, which is the most important thing I have to say, is that I want to come to Mississippi as soon I can and, if it is agreeable with you, to see you for the first time and for you to see and hold your newborn grandson, Kendall Kramer Jr., born on January 10, 1965. I want Kendall to know you as soon as possible. There is one other important thing I want you to know. I am married to a wonderful man, Kendall Kramer Sr., who happens to be white. He knows all about me and you and is proud to have all of us as part of his family. Kendall Sr. would like your permission to come with us to be with you. With Much Love, Your Daughter, Carmen."

After Bobby read the letter, Delmer still seemed to be in a state of shock, and everyone else was completely surprised and happy for Delmer. Instead of making jokes about Delmer, all the men began telling him what he had to do to get ready for the visit from his new family.

Rudy said, "There's not that much getting ready in the world. We need to get some money together to send Delmer to Chicago."

It was agreed that it would be much easier to send Delmer to Chicago, as his house was too small and in too much decline for anyone but Delmer to live in, even for one night.

Rudy added, "Delmer has no means of transportation. He walks everywhere. His family will have to spend a lot of money on themselves and Delmer if they come here."

Delmer said, "I think you boys are right. I know you're right."

"Delmer, we've been friends for a long time. I will go down to the train station and buy you a round-trip ticket. I want the rest of you boys to give as much as you can so Delmer can buy a new suit for his trip and have a little spending money."

"Rudy, I don't know how to thank you and the rest of you fellas. This is the best thing that has ever happened to me."

Mulehead said, "Bobby, you write the letter for Delmer telling his daughter that he has no place for them to stay here, but he would like to come to their home to visit for a week if that's okay with them."

"Yes, sir, Mr. Mulehead."

It took about a month of weekly communication by letter between Delmer and his daughter, with Rudy and Mulehead giving orders to everybody in the barbershop, but finally arrangements were made for Delmer's trip to Chicago in June 1965. It was the happiest moment and week of Delmer's life. All the men in the barbershop agreed that it saved Delmer's life.

CHAPTER 7

THE ROBERT JAMES STORY

Abraham "Sarge" Walters was one of the few younger men who occasionally told an interesting story in the barbershop. Sarge was forty-one years old, six feet four, and weighed 215 pounds. He had served in the army from 1941 to 1945 during World War II and achieved the rank of staff sergeant. He was very proud of this achievement and always wore at least one item of clothing or a cap from his army days. All of Sarge's stories were about his experiences in the army and usually about the time he spent in France. However, the men in the barbershop enjoyed his story about Robert James more than any of his other stories. Sarge and Robert both received training as brick masons while in the army. At 4:00 p.m. on Friday, August 8, 1959, Sarge told his story about Robert James again.

World War II provided an opportunity for us Negro men across the southern United States to obtain a nontraditional education by seeing the world firsthand. We also learned trade skills that would make us employable after the war. While learning valuable trade skills, most of us sent part or even the majority of our military pay home to our wives and families. However, for some wives and families, especially Robert's, what they received was not enough to protect them from the inherent dangers of life that surrounded them.

Robert James was born on February 21, 1922, in Brant, Mississippi, a farm community of about three hundred people near the Mississippi Delta west of Jackson. Odessa Washington, Robert's childhood friend and future wife, was born on May 29, 1922, in Brant. Their parents were sharecroppers with no formal education. However, they had been committed to giving their children an opportunity to have a high school education and refused to allow them to miss any time from school to work on the farms. Their children's education gave their lives purpose and hope. They often told them how proud they were of their good work in school and how blessed they felt to have such smart children who would be able to have better lives far beyond the never-ending work of farm life. Robert and Odessa understood their parents' dreams and hope for them and had great respect for them and the sacrifices they made. This shared awareness and understanding was part of what drew Robert and Odessa into a very close relationship, which soon developed into a serious love for each other.

In late February 1939, Odessa told Robert that she was pregnant. They were in their junior year of high school. Robert and Odessa were both very happy and very sad. They knew that their lives would never be as they, and especially their parents, had planned. Having to tell their parents was the most difficult part of all. Their parents' greatest dream and purpose for working so hard day in and day out since they were married was destroyed.

Robert and Odessa were married on March 15, 1939. Robert was fortunate in that his father had taught him all aspects of farm work, primarily to help motivate him to not want to live such a life for himself. At age seventeen, Robert was also physically able to do the work. He was six feet tall and weighed 190 pounds. He only had to go to the neighboring town of Parkerville to find a farm owner, Grandville Davis, to take him and Odessa as sharecroppers on his fifty-acre farm. Mr. Davis already had two other families working his farm. Because of his size and strength, Mr. Davis decided to give Robert primary responsibility for plowing the fields for planting. Odessa was five feet seven and weighed 120 pounds. When she was twelve her mother explained to her that colored females had to take special care to not attract the attention of white men. She said that colored females were often taken by white men for sex if they so desired. There was no protection for colored females to prevent this from happening. Odessa's mother taught her to cover herself from her neck to her ankles. Odessa never forgot this lesson and always wore large, high-neck collar dresses. Her large dresses served her well at that time to avoid accenting her 34-22-34 frame. Odessa had medium caramel-colored unblemished skin, dark brown eyes, and black hair that extended to the middle of her back. However, she always kept it in a bun and wore a head scarf. She became the personal handmaid to Mr. Davis's youngest daughter, Karen, age eight. Mr. Davis's wife, Rebecca, suffered from a weak heart and passed away shortly after giving birth to Karen.

Odessa gave birth to Gloria May James on September 4, 1939. She was allowed to bring Gloria May to Mr. Davis's house but could only attend to her when it did not interfere with Karen's needs.

On February 11, 1941, Odessa gave birth to a baby boy, Samuel Robert. Samuel's birth was the final motivational push Robert needed to try to revive his and Odessa's parents' dream for a better life for himself and Odessa. Robert and Odessa had been talking about the possibility of Robert joining the army as a way of leaving the sharecropper's life and making a better future for themselves and their children. After the United States declared war on Japan following the bombing of Pearl Harbor on December 7, 1941, the recruiting drive for all branches of the armed forces increased, and Robert informed Mr. Davis that he would like to join the army.

"Mr. Davis, sir, I heard that the country is at war, and I want to do my part. I want to join the army and go and fight. If you give me permission to go I promise to come back when the war is over and work twice as hard for you, especially if you allow my wife and children to stay on your farm while I'm gone."

"Robert, I don't think I like this idea, but I'll go along and let you join the army in January of '43 if sufficient work gets done to ensure a good profit margin for the crops by September of '42."

"I thank you, Mr. Davis, sir, and I will make sure that a lot of work gets done between now and September of '42."

Fortunately for Robert, just the right amount of rain and sunshine occurred during the spring and early summer to produce a bumper crop of cotton, corn, and sugar cane in September 1942.

On January 6, 1943, Robert went to the army recruiting office in Brant.

"Sir, I want to join the army right away and help fight to win the war."

"Well, boy, this is your lucky day because in an hour I'm sending a busload of recruits to Camp Dawson in Crest Ridge, Mississippi. You look okay enough to be sent right away. I'll send all your required exams and tests to Camp Dawson."

Robert boarded the bus at 11:00 a.m. and at 1:30 p.m. arrived at Camp Dawson to be officially enlisted into the army and begin basic training.

Completing thirteen weeks of basic training was challenging but not too difficult for Robert, as he was physically very strong and in great condition. On the firing range he made marksman in record time. He was given the nickname "Sergeant York" after the World War I hero, Sergeant Alvin York, who became famous for his marksmanship at the battle in Argonne Forest in France on October 8, 1918. Robert was proud of his efforts to give his best at everything he was asked to do. The untiring and long-suffering commitment of his and Odessa's parents was never far from his consciousness. Nor was his desire to make their dreams come true through the lives of Gloria May and Samuel Robert.

Robert received fifty dollars per month as a private in the army and would usually send at least thirty dollars home to Odessa. He knew Odessa would use what was necessary and save as much as possible for their future away from Mr. Davis's farm. Robert also realized that he needed a more financially productive way to support his family when he returned home. He was always good with his hands and took every opportunity to spend time at the motor pool watching the mechanics work on the army vehicles. He also was drawn to the carpenters and brick masons because he admired their knowledge and skills, and the pride they took in the artistry of their work. They told Robert that when other people saw their work, they wanted them to see something of beauty as well as of purpose. Robert could see and feel their pride. It was a feeling that he wanted for himself, and, equally as important, these were skilled professions that paid far better than farming someone else's land. The carpenters and brick masons appreciated Robert's desire to learn and improve his life. They were glad to teach him what they knew. Before basic training ended, Robert decided that he preferred brick masonry over carpentry because he found the effort of working with bricks and concrete more challenging.

Robert was always very careful when he sent money home to Odessa. He was afraid that if Mr. Davis found out how much he was sending and that Odessa was saving as much as possible, he might suspect that they were planning to leave the farm and would demand payment in lost income for the time Robert had been away. He and Odessa agreed that if Mr. Davis were to ever ask if he was sending money home to her, Odessa would tell him that her husband was not very good with money and was only sending her about ten dollars every month or two. Odessa also took great care in making sure that she did not buy anything for herself or her children that would attract Mr. Davis' attention.

Odessa worked very hard every day attending to the needs of Mr. Davis's daughter, Karen, in addition to trying to give as much attention to Gloria May and Samuel Robert as she could. Odessa had sectioned off a portion of the kitchen where she kept Gloria May and Samuel Robert. Now twelve years old, Karen was a loving child and never hesitated to speak her mind. It was common practice during that time that white children cared for by Negro housekeepers called their caretakers aunt and uncle. Karen called Odessa "auntie."

"Auntie, you are so busy all the time. I'm going to help you take care of Gloria May and Samuel Robert."

"Thank you, Miss Karen, but you don't have to do that. I can take care of them all right."

Odessa was concerned that Mr. Davis would consider it very inappropriate if not insulting for his daughter to assist in the care of his colored housekeeper's children.

"But, Auntie, you don't understand. I have to start learning how to take care of a house and children so I'll know what to do when I get married and have my own children."

"That's mighty fine, Miss Karen, but I think your daddy might not like your idea, and he just might get upset with me for letting you do such a thing."

The next morning when Odessa arrived at Mr. Davis's house, she was met in the kitchen by Mr. Davis and Karen.

"Odessa, Karen tells me that she wants to start learning how to take care of things around here because one day she will be a wife and mother. You teach her what she wants to know."

"Yes, sir, Mr. Davis."

"Another thing, old Martha is seventy years of age now and no longer able to keep up with my washing and ironing needs and the making of my special meals; you will take over for her in addition to taking care of Karen. This means you will need to come a little earlier and stay a little longer each day."

"Yes, sir, Mr. Davis."

"I'm leaving now, and I will be back around dinnertime. You do a good job of teaching Karen what she needs to know, Odessa."

"Yes, sir, Mr. Davis, I'll do that."

"Now Auntie, you don't have to worry about Daddy being upset."

In spite of having a longer workday, Odessa felt some relief about being able to spend a little more time attending to Gloria May and Samuel Robert. At least as long as Karen was interested in learning how to be a wife and mother.

For the first two months Odessa felt very tired at the end of the day and then having to carry two sleeping children home to their cabin. Fortunately, Karen had not yet lost interest in becoming a wife and mother, which enabled Odessa to regularly look in on Gloria May and Samuel Robert. She made sure that when Karen returned home from school each day, she had her change into play clothes and have a sandwich and soup before doing her homework and then learning another lesson about being a wife and mother. Odessa could not help caring very much for Karen. She had a kind and generous spirit. Odessa hoped that Karen would always be able to see everyone as a person worthy of treatment no different from every other person.

At age twenty-one and after giving birth to two children, Odessa had returned to her prepregnancy weight and shape. On May 21, 1943, Mr. Granville Davis celebrated his thirty-third birthday. He enjoyed giving parties at his estate and particularly on his birthday. Mr. Davis's neighbors sent their best cooks to him three days before his birthday to help Odessa prepare the food. The party would start at 3:00 p.m. and would not end until daybreak the following morning.

As usual, everyone had arrived by 5:00 p.m., including Mr. Davis's neighbors, friends, business leaders, city and state politicians, and all their family members. The party was in full force. There were about seventy people at the party. Odessa and the members of both of the other sharecropper families on Mr. Davis's farm served the food and drinks to Mr. Davis's guests. Martha was not needed at the party and kept Gloria May and Samuel Robert in her cabin for Odessa.

Everyone was having a very enjoyable time at the party. Around 1:00 a.m., Odessa was starting to feel exhausted and needed to get off her feet for a few minutes. She decided to go upstairs to the bathroom at the end of the hall opposite Mr. Davis's bedroom. As she had hoped, that bathroom was unoccupied. Odessa decided she would spend no more than ten minutes in the bathroom. She took off the special servant's dress that Mr. Davis provided so she could feel more comfortable. About a minute later the bathroom door opened. It was Mr. Davis. He had also felt tired and had gone to his bedroom for an hour's nap. He was now about ready to return to the party. When Mr. Davis saw Odessa, it was as though he was seeing her for the first time. His surprise quickly turned to awareness and then to desire. He was completely taken with her physical beauty. Odessa was angry with herself for not taking the time to lock the door.

"Mr. Davis, sir, I am so sorry for using this bathroom. I was real tired and needed to rest for a little. I'm putting my dress right back on and going right back to work at the party."

"Before you go back downstairs come to my room. I want to talk to you about Karen. Bring your dress. You can put it on in my room."

"Yes, sir, Mr. Davis. I'll be right there."

When they entered his bedroom Mr. Davis took the dress from Odessa and threw it on a chair. He then took Odessa into his arms.

"Odessa, I never realized how beautiful you were. I want you to consider my attraction to you as just another part of your job."

"Yes, sir, Mr. Davis."

This encounter became the first of many regular sexual encounters that Odessa was required to have with Mr. Davis.

Odessa was torn between her loyalty and commitment to her husband and the reality that there was no one she could turn to for help, and there was no place she could go and be any better off than she was with Mr. Davis. The greater likelihood was that she would be subject to much more abuse with a different farm owner. Her mother had told her about other black women sharecroppers who were abused by every male member of the farm owner's family, and even their male friends, on a regular basis. Odessa decided to behave as normally as she could and pray that Robert would return home soon, and they could leave Mr. Davis's farm for a home of their own.

After each sexual encounter with Mr. Davis, Odessa would quickly wash herself thoroughly to try to prevent an unwanted pregnancy. However, in September 1943, Odessa knew that her period was about one week late. She did not want to worry unnecessarily because her period had been late by a few days before. Odessa did begin to worry when her period did not come at all in September or October. On November 1, 1943, she was certain she was pregnant and shared this information with Mr. Davis after Karen had gone to bed for the night.

"Mr. Davis, I want you to know, sir, that I am pregnant with your child."

"Odessa, that's no real concern of mine, but if you want an abortion I will get the doctor over here to do it for you. It might be a good idea, and that way you would never have to tell Robert about it when he returns. If you decide to have the child I won't take any responsibility for it or acknowledgment for its existence and you won't say otherwise."

"Yes, sir, Mr. Davis."

Odessa considered Mr. Davis's offer of an abortion, but could not bring herself to see this as a real option for her, given her strong religious beliefs about the sanctity of life. She would have the child but would not share this information with Robert until his return, as she wanted Robert to devote all his efforts to keeping himself safe and able to return home.

Odessa never felt that Mr. Davis treated her badly. He never beat her or caused her children to be endangered by his desires for her. He was actually very polite and considerate of her in public. As Karen grew older, Odessa's motherly relationship with her continued to grow. Mr. Davis did nothing to negatively affect their relationship and seemed to appreciate Odessa's very caring attitude toward Karen.

On April 18, 1944, Odessa gave birth to a baby girl. She named the baby Deloris after her grandmother. Odessa's mother told her many times about the multitude of problems her own mother had to face in her life, and somehow she survived them all. Odessa knew that her little Deloris would need the same kind of inner strength and perseverance of her namesake to live the kind of life that lay before her. Odessa knew that little Deloris would be considered a mulatto and probably not be welcomed in the Negro or white community. Her only place of real acceptance would be in the home that she and Robert would make for her. Her family and God would be little Deloris's only, but also greatest, source of strength.

Robert completed his service in the army on October 15, 1945, and returned to Mr. Davis's farm in Parkerville,

Mississippi. He was confident that with his skills as a brick mason and the job references he was given by his instructors, he would be able to make a decent living and provide a good and safe home for his family far from Mr. Davis's farm. Prior to his arrival, on August 23, 1945, Odessa gave birth to her second child by Mr. Davis. Odessa named her baby boy Clayton. Clayton was the name of Odessa's maternal uncle, whose skin color and physical features were clearly more white than Negro. Her uncle Clayton left Mississippi at the age of sixteen, moved to New Orleans, and lived as a white man. Mr. Davis was awestruck by how much Odessa's little Clayton reminded him of how Karen looked at her birth. Little Clayton's skin was as white as Mr. Davis's, and he had no Negro features.

As Odessa had hoped and prayed, Robert listened with love and understanding to the story of her life since he left for the army on January 6, 1943.

"Odessa, I thank God that you survived and managed to take care of all our children. My love and respect for you has increased because of your faith and courage. Our future has been made possible by your sacrifice and undying commitment to our love, our dreams, and our parents' dreams. My hope is that our children might be able to live in a world where such extreme sacrifices will no longer have to be made."

CHAPTER 8

THE PHILIP MICHAEL WIGGINS STORY

Whenever Preacher Casey came to the barbershop he had a parable to tell about God's ultimate victory over evil, particularly the Ku Klux Klan, since it was undisputedly the root of most of the evils Negroes faced on a daily basis. Preacher Casey's wife, Nellie, worked for thirty years in the home of Warren Taylor Wiggins and Helen Wiggins. Almost every night she had a new story to tell Preacher about the Wiggins family. One Saturday afternoon in March 1976, Preacher told the men what Nellie had told him about Philip Michael.

Philip Michael Wiggins was born on September 10, 1938, in Crabtree, Mississippi. Crabtree was a small town with a population of about one thousand and was best known for its cotton fields. While Crabtree and several of the surrounding small towns were farming communities, their biggest farm product and primary source of income was cotton.

Philip's parents, Warren Taylor and Helen Wiggins, owned a ninety-acre farm. Eighty acres were devoted to growing cotton, which over the years had consistently been financially productive. The Wiggins had a six-bedroom home that included a library and entertainment room complete with a grand piano and full bar. Philip had a younger sister, Jennifer Kay, who was born on February 6, 1940.

When Philip reached the age of ten, he started to realize that everyone did not have a home, clothes, and toys similar to his own. His school classmates' homes that he and his parents visited were not that different from his own. He liked his classmates well enough, but he enjoyed playing with the two children of the colored sharecropper families that worked on his family's farm much more. Philip considered Daniel Sampson, age ten, and Elizabeth Rogers, age nine, his best friends. He learned songs from them that they sang in their church and learned how to tell ghost stories. They always played together in Philip's front yard.

On a Saturday morning in June while playing in the yard, Daniel's mother called for him to come home for a while to do some chores. Philip suggested to Elizabeth that they walk home with Daniel and hurry him along with his chores so they could get back to their games. When they arrived at Daniel's home, Philip thought it was a one-room storage shed, as it seemed to be the same size as the storage shed near his family's barn. He decided not to ask Daniel if he and Elizabeth could come inside because he did not want Daniel to feel bad about not having a nice house in which to live. Philip and Elizabeth played tag in the yard while they waited for Daniel.

Philip also started to observe his parents' activities and pay more attention to their attitudes and instructions, particularly about colored people. He understood that his parents felt that whites had their roles in life, which were primarily as leaders and Negroes had roles primarily as workers and servants. Philip knew that his father occasionally attended Ku Klux Klan meetings, but he always treated everyone fairly. His father told him often how important it was for Negroes to remember their place in society because this was part of God's plan for mankind. It was the duty of whites to help Negroes understand God's will.

Philip had always found his father's beliefs and instructions about the roles of whites and Negroes to be very entertaining, much in the same way as the ghost stories he learned from Daniel and Elizabeth. He had not yet felt that they had any relevance in his life other than the need to show respect for his father.

On September 10, 1951, when Philip turned thirteen, his father gave him his first rifle, a lightweight .22-caliber gun.

"Son, it's time for you to begin your development to manhood and your role as a leader. You and I are going to spend time each day practicing with your rifle until you can practice on your own. Also, and just as important, you will no longer consider Daniel and Elizabeth your friends or your equals. They are the employees of the farm, as are their parents."

"Couldn't I spend time with Daniel and Elizabeth anyway, even if they can no longer be my friends?"

"You can speak to them as necessary and particularly to give them instructions about work or anything else you want them to do. Behaving as though they were your friends could give them the impression that they were your equal. This is a very important lesson you must learn and remember. All niggers must understand that they are not your equal and that they must stay in their place. Your friends will be boys and girls from the good white families in Crabtree."

"Yes, Daddy."

Philip realized that he must always show respect for his father, but his heart and mind told him that the whole idea of white supremacy did not make much sense. Everything he had seen and experienced thus far demonstrated to him that colored people worked very hard every day, made the most of whatever they had without complaining, were very respectful, honest, helpful to anyone who needed help, talented, God fearing, and loved their families. Philip could not think of anything white people had or demonstrated that would make them better human beings or leaders. He decided that he must be too young to understand what his father had been trying to explain to him.

At the age of thirteen Philip attended a Klan meeting with is father. His father told him that he needed to understand how other boys his age were learning about their roles in society. At the end of the meeting Philip did not feel he had heard anything that his father had not already told him.

Once outside, Philip and the other boys who had attended the meeting began to talk to each other. Philip was anxious to find out if the other boys had a better understanding about the possible destruction of the white race that the men seemed to fear that could be caused by Negroes if they did not stay in their place. Mitchell Bodie, a sixteen-year-old, said that he was looking forward to the day he would become a member of the Klan and get a white robe and hat.

"Mitchell, do you know what had happened to make our fathers believe that the white race was in danger of being destroyed?"

"Philip, the problem goes back to slavery and the Civil War. The South lost the Civil War, and Lincoln let the niggers out of their rightful place as slaves. Now they think they can be equal to us, and they don't even know that they aren't even real humans."

"Philip, did your father ever tell you that the niggers are only three-fifths human?"

"I don't remember him ever saying that, Mitchell."

"If you don't believe me you can look it up because it was the law, and there were many other laws that protected white people from niggers. But since a lot of niggers couldn't read, they broke the law all the time without realizing what they were doing. My dad told me that a lot of the old laws were never changed, so a lot of niggers are still breaking the law. If the white race allows the niggers to become equals, they will start marrying white women and the next thing you know, there won't be any more real white people, and worse than that, we won't even be real humans anymore. The Klan has to keep all this from happening."

"Mitchell, do you hate colored people?"

"Naw, I don't hate them. They never done nothing to me. I guess I get along with them as well as I get along with anybody else, but that's not the point. Everything would be all right if niggers just stayed in their place. Most of them are sharecroppers anyway, and they would probably be happier if they could be slaves again and not have to worry about all the problems real humans have to worry about."

Philip never told Mitchell or the other boys or anyone else that he could not see what made colored people any less human than white people.

In May 1956, Philip graduated from Crabtree High School. Both his parents were graduates of Orion State University in Plum Hill, Mississippi, so Philip had known since tenth grade that he would be attending Orion as well. Philip had looked forward to his college career and to one day becoming a lawyer. His parents were proud of his desire to become a lawyer, but they did not know that Philip's interest in the law was sparked by Mitchell Bodie's statements to him after his first Klan meeting.

Philip had continued his friendship with Daniel and Elizabeth against his father's wishes. He told Daniel and Elizabeth what his father had said about them.

"I want y'all to know that I love and respect my father, but I don't think he and the Klan are right about what they believe about colored people. You both have been my best friends since I can remember, and I don't want that to ever change."

"We feel the same way about you, Philip, and we will never tell anyone that you are our friend."

Philip gave his best effort to understand his father's beliefs and commitment to the work of the Ku Klux Klan on behalf of all white people, but his own mind and experience, particularly with Daniel and Elizabeth and their families, did not lead him to accept the paranoia and hate necessary to make a commitment to the Ku Klux Klan.

Philip did exceptionally well at Orion. He graduated with a 4.0 grade point average in June 1960. His major was political science and his minor was in economics. He remained at Orion for his law degree, which he received in 1963.

Philip had many successes in his life, which he realized would have not been possible without the resources and support of his family. He often wondered how successful Daniel and Elizabeth might have been if their parents had been able to give them the advantages he received. Philip always believed that both Daniel and Elizabeth were innately more intelligent and creative than he. Daniel's and Elizabeth's formal education ended in the eighth grade, as their parents needed them to help with their work responsibilities. They married each other and remained on the Wiggins farm as sharecroppers.

After working for a corporate tax law firm in Fort Green, Mississippi, for two years, Philip told his father that he would open his own corporate tax law office in 1965. His father wanted him to return to Crabtree to open his law office but realized that Fort Green was a far better location for the kind of law Philip wanted to practice. Philip continued to tell his father that one day he would try to make time to catch up on all the news his father wanted to share with him about the Klan. He did not share with his father that he would be starting trust funds for Daniel and Elizabeth's four children to ensure that they would receive college educations.

On a visit to see his parents, Philip also visited Daniel and Elizabeth.

"I want you both to know that it makes me very happy to set up the trust funds for your children's college education. They deserve a chance in life. I want you to find a way to get word to me if you have any needs or concerns about keeping your children in grade school or in preparing for them to attend college."

"Philip, we don't know how to thank you or repay your kindness. All we can say is thank-you."

Philip hoped that his support of Daniel and Elizabeth's children would result in their ability to make a contribution toward the effort by all colored people on a very difficult road toward equality.

Philip also served from 1965 to 1975 in the Fort Green Poverty Law Center. Philip's father rarely spoke to him after Philip told him that he had made a major time commitment to the work of the Fort Green Poverty Law Center. He tried to explain to his father that he loved him dearly and would always appreciate everything he and his mother had done for him. However, one of the lessons they had possibly unintentionally taught him was that every child, regardless of their race or color, needed that same kind of love and support if they were to have the best opportunity for a successful life. To deliberately devise a system to deny any parents the possibility of providing an opportunity for their children to be successful was not something a moral society should tolerate.

Philip's mother told him, "Son, I always knew that there was something different about you. From childhood I was taught and accepted everything your father believes in, especially the philosophy of the Ku Klux Klan. But since your first Klan meeting, I could look in your eyes and know that your heart and mind would never allow you to accept such ideas and beliefs."

CHAPTER 9

THE HOWARD BROWN STORY

Page "Slim" Fuller was about seventy-five years old, five feet seven, weighed about 200 pounds, and was completely bald. The men in the barbershop said it was a miracle that Slim had lived to be seventy-five years old since he was so short and as far as anyone knew, had been overweight all his life. Slim denied having been overweight all his life, as he claimed to have been a Pullman porter for ten years. Slim said everyone knew that Pullman porters were not overweight. No one could deny that Slim seemed to know a lot about Pullman porters. In the barbershop on a hot August afternoon in 1968, he told the story of Howard Brown.

In 1927, Howard Brown applied to become a Pullman porter. Howard was single, twenty-five years old, six feet two, and weighed 215 pounds, and he lived on the South Side of Chicago. At the time, a large number of Pullman porters lived on Chicago's South Side. Since the age of twelve, Howard admired the Pullman porters in his neighborhood and wanted to become one as soon as he could. From the age of nine, Howard stood out among his friends and classmates because he was taller and bigger than everyone else. Because of his size at age sixteen, five feet eleven and 190 pounds, he was able to get work at construction sites in addition to other odd jobs. He continued to do construction work and odd jobs throughout the city of Chicago, always hoping for an opportunity to become a Pullman porter.

Howard loved talking to his next-door neighbor, Ronald Jones, who had been a Pullman porter for three years. Howard enjoyed listening to Mr. Jones talk about his travels on the trains. Every time he saw Mr. Jones, he would remind him that he wanted his help to become a Pullman porter.

"Good afternoon, Mr. Jones. You look like you are in a hurry. Are you getting ready to go on another trip?"

"Yes, I am, Howard. I'm on my way to the train now."

"Well, you have a good trip, Mr. Jones, and don't forget that I want to be a Pullman porter too."

"Sure, Howard, sure. I'll do my best to help you."

Howard was almost shocked the day Mr. Jones rushed home to tell him that one of the porters had suffered an injury to his leg that would prevent him from continuing on a scheduled trip to California.

"Howard, I asked my friend in the union personnel office for a special favor. I told him that I knew there were others ahead of you on the list of candidates for potential hire, but I assured him that you would be able to come to the train station immediately and would not delay the train's scheduled departure time from Chicago en route to California. My friend agreed to try you out on this trip because he did not want the train to be late because of a problem with the porters. If things go well, he may give you consideration for an apprentice membership in the union."

"Mr. Jones, I don't know how to thank you for giving me this opportunity except to say that I will do my very best."

Howard had a very successful trip to California. He followed Mr. Jones's instructions and worked as hard as he could to please the passengers and the staff. They were all impressed with the quality as well as the quantity of his work. One week after the trip, Howard received a letter stating that he was accepted as an apprentice Pullman porter.

Howard was employed as a Pullman porter for forty years. He retired in 1957 at the age of sixty-five. One of his most memorable passengers that he regularly served was Stanley Wilson.

In 1940 Stanley Wilson was forty years old, five feet ten, and weighed about 180 pounds. He had played halfback on his college football team and had always been mindful about his health and weight, so he was not in bad shape for a forty-year-old.

Stanley was a hardware store owner who had a girlfriend and family in each of the cities where his hardware stores were located. He owned very successful hardware stores in Detroit, Michigan; Miami, Florida; and Austin, Texas. He had attended the University of Miami and received a degree in business administration. He enjoyed traveling between his stores and did so of necessity as often as he could. His hardware stores were well managed, but it was not always easy managing three families. Stanley had to be very careful about his situation, and he took great pains to speak of his families as little as possible to his associates. Howard was one of the Pullman porters that Stanley felt he could talk to and trust not to reveal any of his secrets. For these private and privileged conversations, Stanley would tip Howard one hundred dollars at the end of each journey.

"Howard, boy, I actually started my families quite accidently. One night in Detroit in July 1940, after meeting with supply company representatives and my store managers, I was too tired to go to my hotel room and go to bed. I decided to go to a fancy nightclub, watch a show, and order the biggest porterhouse steak in the kitchen. I had been to this club before, but that night I had a waitress that I had not seen before."

"Hello, gorgeous, my name is Stanley Wilson," I said. "I'm a wealthy businessman spending time in Detroit overseeing one of my many hardware stores. How would you like to join me after your shift is over?"

"My name is Carol Allen," she said. "My shift is over in an hour, and I will come and join you then."

"That's wonderful, Carol," I replied. "Be sure to order yourself a porterhouse steak and add it to my bill."

"Well, thank you, Mr. Wilson," Carol answered. "I'll do just that."

"Call me Stanley," I said.

"I'm Carol," she responded.

"Howard, boy, Carol was appreciative for the meal because she was an aspiring actress and was saving her money to create a portfolio to send to Hollywood and New York in hopes of landing a modeling or acting job. She was really gorgeous. She was twenty-three years old, five feet four, and weighed about 110 pounds, with shoulder-length, red hair. She was a native of Detroit but spent as much time as she could sunbathing in the park. Her striking, even tan gave quite a contrast to her red hair."

"We continued talking long after our meal. At 4:00 a.m. I offered to treat Carol to a room at the Four Seasons Hotel where I was staying for the week."

"Carol, it has been so nice talking with you." I said. "I would love to continue, but it's 4:00 a.m., and we both could use some sleep. Why don't you let me treat you to a nice room at The Four Seasons where I'm staying? And don't worry; there are 'no strings attached' to my offer. I simply admire your dedication and hard work and feel that you deserve a nice break."

"Thank you again, Stanley," she said. "I'm sure that if you had other intentions you have enough money to get a date with a well-known socialite."

"Howard boy, the next day I asked Carol to spend the rest of the week at the hotel and I offered her more money than she was making in the nightclub to work for me in my hardware store."

"Carol, I'm really glad you accepted my job offer because it will be very gratifying for me to know that I will be helping you achieve your goal of becoming an actress," I said.

"Stanley, you have made me so happy I don't know what to say," Carol replied. "I do want to ask one thing of you. Please let me spend the rest of the week in your room. I know you did not and would not ask me to, but I want to so much."

"Okay, Carol. I could never say no to you," I answered.

"Howard, boy, Carol and I had a great time that week. I left Detroit on Sunday morning and went to Miami, where I owned a three-bedroom house and two hardware stores. I told Carol that I would probably return to Detroit in November around Thanksgiving for another visit. I gave her my primary office telephone number and told her to call and leave a message if necessary, and I would return her call as soon as I could. Otherwise, I would see her again in November."

"In Miami I had been living with my girlfriend, Debra Bradford, since 1937. Debra was a graduate of the University of Florida with an accounting degree, and she worked as the business manager for my two hardware stores. Debra was thirty-eight years old, five feet six, and 115 pounds, with blonde hair that she liked to keep short and manageable. Debra had been married previously and had two children—a son, Adam, age seventeen, and a daughter, Anne, age fifteen. While she managed to support herself and her children and lived in her own apartment, I told her that I was committed to her and her children and they were welcome to stay in my home anytime. I told Debra that I admired her independence and that one day when I did not have to travel so much I would ask her to marry me."

"Howard, boy, Debra never knew and never asked why I needed to spend between one and two weeks when I visited my other stores. I think it was because I always came through when she asked me for help with any of her family issues. I had always been especially helpful when she needed a man to talk with Adam about his problems and concerns. I think she felt this unwavering dependability earned me her trust, so she never asked questions."

"I really did care a lot for Debra and her two children, and I was always glad to help them, but I was never sure about marrying Debra. Howard, boy, the best way to ruin a good relationship with a woman is to marry her. Did you know that?"

"Well, boss, I don't know what I thought before, but I'm glad I understand about marriage now."

Howard said he actually liked Stanley more than most of the other passengers during his years on the train, mainly because Stanley always called him and the other porters by their actual names and not "George" like the company told the passengers to do.

"Howard, boy, in September of 1940, I told Debra that I needed to go to my Austin, Texas, store for one week to meet with the store managers about inventory needs and financial reports that would soon be needed for tax reporting. I never liked spending more than one week at a time in Austin, mainly because of my girlfriend of two years at that time,

Mary 'Annie' Oakley. I wanted to break it off with Mary after I really got to know her, but I didn't know how."

"I met Mary one day at a liquor store in Austin. I had stopped in the store to pick up a bottle of my favorite scotch and some cigars to take to my hotel room. As I was turning at the end of an aisle, Mary was coming from the other direction, and we bumped into each other. Neither of us was hurt by the collision, but Mary found it very funny when I bounced off her into a cigar display. Mary was twenty-eight years old, six feet one, and weighed 170 pounds. She was raised on her family's cattle ranch outside of Abilene, where she grew up riding horse and shooting .45-caliber six-guns with her three older brothers. After bouncing off the cigar display, I did not want to appear weak or embarrassed by her laughter, so I began laughing along with her."

"Well, sir, I must say that I am impressed with your self-confidence," the woman said. "Most men shy away from me and the rest run away, especially the ones who are shorter and smaller. If you really do have self-confidence why don't you let me take you to dinner?"

"I would love to go," I said. "I rarely get a dinner invitation from a beautiful woman."

"I knew I was going a bit overboard with that comment, but I wanted Mary to remember that I was one of the few real men she had ever met, especially one that was smaller than she."

"Mary took me to a steakhouse, where she ordered porterhouse steak and lobster for both of us. After a great meal and learning all about her life on her family's cattle ranch, I thanked Mary for a very enjoyable evening."

"Stanley, this has been a most enjoyable evening for me as well," Mary said. "You are a lot of fun to be with. How long will you be in Austin?"

"I have to leave Friday morning to go to Miami, and I have to prepare for tomorrow's business meetings, so I need to get back to my hotel now." I replied. "If you give me your address and phone number I will call you when I return to Austin."

"That's a good idea, Stanley," she said. "Let me borrow your pen."

"Howard, boy, when I came down to the front desk Friday at 8:00 a.m., there stood Mary."

"Good morning, Stanley," she said. "I decided that you have to come to Abilene with me to see the ranch before you go back to Miami. And, since it's Friday, you have to spend the weekend. I promise you will have a wonderful time."

"Before I could collect my thoughts and say something, Mary picked up my suitcase."

"Come on, my car is out front with the motor running," she said.

"Howard, boy, that was some weekend. Mary found a very tame horse for me to ride, and she showed me the whole 250 acres and all her guns. Mary rode her horse like it was as comfortable as a cloud. She handled her .45-caliber six-guns like they were extensions of her fingers. After dinner that Friday night, I was wiped out and was glad to see the king-size bed in the bedroom that was provided for me."

"After sleeping completely through the night, Saturday began at 8:00 a.m. with a Texas-size breakfast—a sixteen-ounce porterhouse steak with eggs, buttermilk biscuits with onion gravy, and a sixteen-ounce glass of 24 percent butterfat milk. I was surprised that I was able to consume the entire meal and felt amazingly satisfied afterwards. The rest of Saturday was spent getting to know more about Mary and her family, and, of course, getting the whole story about why her brothers nicknamed her 'Annie.' By then I really didn't need any more information about her nickname, as the things I watched her do on Friday made her nickname clear and appropriate. The only mystery was why her parents did not name her Annie rather than Mary in the first place. I'm sure that the real Annie Oakley could not have had any more abilities or skills with a horse and six-gun than Mary."

"By bedtime Saturday night, I felt that I was having a good time, but I was ready to get back to Miami on Sunday. At about 10:30 p.m., after another fine Texas meal and thanking Mary and her family for a wonderful weekend, I went to my room. As I did the night before, I was asleep in ten minutes."

"At 12:30 a.m., I felt myself being gently awakened. It was Mary. She had climbed into my bed and was nude."

"Stanley, I could not let the weekend end without showing you how much I enjoyed having you here and making me feel so comfortable around you," Mary said.

"I really did not need for Mary to show me that much appreciation, so I tried to convince her that while I was very flattered and otherwise would welcome her special thank-you, it would probably be best for her to return to her room before other family members realized that we were together, especially since I knew that I would not be able to keep the noise level down."

"Don't worry, Stanley, all my family members are very sound sleepers and would only notice if the roof fell on them," Mary said. "Besides, I brought this along to be sure we are not disturbed."

"Mary showed me one of her .45-caliber six-guns, which she laid on the night table. Howard, boy, I tell you when I saw that big gun I was scared near to death. I lost my words and just did whatever Mary said at that point. The fact that she continued to smile caused me not to panic. After our romp in the hay, which I have to tell you, Howard, boy, was pretty exceptional, Mary picked up the gun, started waving it around and laughing, and told me what a stud I was."

"What's the matter, Stanley?" Mary asked. "You are so quiet now. You didn't think this gun was loaded, did you?"

"Well, Mary," I said, "I didn't know if it was or not."

"That's when she laughed so hard I thought she would wake up her family. She then showed me the empty bullet chambers."

"Dear Stanley, I promise not to ever do anything like this again," Mary said. "I swear I would never do anything to harm you. I really feel terrible about this. You have to let me make this up to you."

"Howard, boy, it was at that point that I knew I was in trouble. I took my first real look at Mary, the way a man usually looks at a woman. Mary had big brown eyes with natural lashes that seemed an inch or more long, dark brown hair that she always wore in a tight bun so I did not know it went down to her waist, and she had a figure that would put an hourglass to shame. I stopped being afraid of Mary and started wanting to be with her as often as I could. Over the next three years I was still sure that I did not want to end my relationship with her. I came to realize that Mary had as good or better chance than Carol and Debra of becoming my wife if I could ever ask anyone to have that role."

"Howard, boy, things went well with Mary, Carol, and Debra until January 1942. As usual, I had planned to spend the month of January at my home in Miami because I did not like cold weather. After making time to call Mary and Carol to express my regrets about not being able to be with them to welcome the New Year, I treated Debra to a night on the town and later joined friends to share the New Year's celebration. The next day Debra told me that before I woke up she had received a message that her mother was ill in Tampa, Florida, and she needed to pick up her children and go to Tampa as soon as possible. I told her to call me if I could be of help, as I had taken the week off from work and decided I would just stay at home and take it easy."

"Howard, boy, at 12 noon on January 3, 1942, there was a knock at my front door. I answered the door, and, to my complete surprise, there was Mary. All six feet one and

170 pounds. I was speechless because I had not extended an invitation for her to come for a visit, and she had never made surprise visits in the past."

"Hello, Stanley!" Mary said. "Surprised to see me, I'll bet. But don't worry, I don't plan to stay long because I know you are busy and may not have much time for me on a surprise visit."

"That's actually very true, Mary," I said. "I have a lot of work to do."

"I understand and I will only stay for a day or two and not interfere with anything you had planned to do," she replied.

"I was really glad to hear this because Debra would be away for a week or so, which will not make it look like I am rushing her away."

"Stanley, I missed you very much, and I felt that I needed to show you that I was willing to make whatever sacrifice necessary for our relationship to work," Mary said.

"Howard, boy, I think because Mary was thirty years old, she was worried about not being able to have children if she did not marry soon."

"Mary, I really appreciate and respect what you're telling me, and I will give it very serious thought," I said. "However, in the future I need for you to plan your visits with me mainly because I have to travel a lot, and there is no guarantee that I would be home when you might arrive for a surprise visit."

"I realized that, Stanley, but it was a risk I was willing to take this time, particularly since it was the first surprise visit I have ever made to see you during our four-year relationship," Mary answered.

"Mary, I'm going to make as much time for you today as possible, but I won't have any time tomorrow, as I will be very busy," I said. "Follow me, and I'll take you to a spare guest bedroom so you can freshen up and relax for a few minutes before we go out."

"Howard, boy, the next morning Mary told me how much she appreciated the day and night before. She realized she had disrupted my work schedule, so she would be leaving on the noon train returning to Abilene. I was greatly relieved to hear this. I thanked her for coming and promised to give a lot of thought to her need to have a permanent relationship and a family."

"When I waved good-bye to Mary from the train platform, I knew I had been very lucky. I had no idea what I would have said to Debra and Mary if Debra had been in the house when Mary arrived. I had never seen Debra, Mary, or Carol angry, and I was not anxious to find out what they would be like. I decided that I would need to rethink my Austin/Abilene visit schedule to prevent Mary from feeling the need to make surprise visits. I also needed to make a decision about Mary's need to have a family of her own."

"To give myself a chance to think, I decided to go to Detroit to see Carol. I wrote a note to Debra and left it in her home mailbox stating that I needed to make an emergency trip to the Detroit store, but would probably return home in a few days. I arrived in Detroit on Friday night, January 5, 1942. I decided to spend a quiet night in my hotel room and see Carol the next morning at the hardware store."

"I arrived at the hardware store Saturday around 10:00 a.m. After meeting with one of my store managers, I walked over to the cash register where Carol was working and told her that I would return to the store at the close of the day and would take her to dinner. I returned to the store in a cab at 7:00 p.m. and waited for Carol to exit. When she came out of the store I waved to her, and she ran over to the cab."

"Hello, Carol," I said. "I can't find the words to tell you how much I have missed you. I missed you so much that I changed my mind about taking you out to dinner. I decided to order our dinner and have it brought to my hotel room. I ordered our usual porterhouse steak, baked potato, and garden salad."

"That sounds wonderful, Stanley." Carol said. "I'm looking forward to it as always."

"As we were beginning to get ready to share some intimate time in bed, Carol realized that she had left her purse with her money and apartment keys in the hardware store."

"Stanley, could I borrow your master key to the hardware store and get my purse?" Carol asked.

"Sure, Carol," I said. "Here's the key and some money for a cab to get you there and back."

"Thank you so much, Stanley. I'll be back as soon as I can," she said.

"Howard, boy, no more than five minutes after Carol left there was a knock at the door. I opened the door, and there was Mary. She shocked me even more when the first thing she did was shout that she was so excited and happy; she had just found out that afternoon that she was pregnant, and she just couldn't wait to tell me."

"Stanley, Stanley, oh Stanley, I'm pregnant!" Mary said. "As soon as my doctor told me I ran home and told my family. They were excited to hear the news, but they could only take so much of my very loud and expressive happiness. They all told me that I needed to tell you the good news right away, and I needed to tell you in person. I told them that I had promised you that I would not make any more surprise visits to see you and that I was going to call your office and leave a message for you to call me, but they said that this was an exceptional situation which you would want to know about as soon as possible, and in person. I called your office and was told that you were in Detroit at a business meeting, but they would not tell me the name of the hotel where you were staying. I went to the train station and purchased a ticket to Detroit. When I arrived I began going to the best hotels near the train station and asking if Stanley Wilson was registered, telling the desk clerks that I was Mrs. Stanley Wilson. It only took going to two hotels before I found you."

"Before I could say anything to Mary, I watched her reach into her purse and pull out one of her .45-caliber six-guns."

"Stanley, do you remember this gun?" she asked.

"Yes, Mary, I remember the gun." I said.

"Remember I told you that night it was not loaded?" she continued.

"Yes," I answered.

"Well, it is loaded now in honor of my pregnancy, which was made possible because you are a super stud, just like my .45-caliber six-gun is much more than just an average handgun. Stanley, are you happy that I am pregnant?" she said.

"Yes, I'm very happy." I responded.

"Stanley, I also remember that I promised to never do anything to hurt you," she said. "I'm going to put my gun over on the table by the door and show you how happy I am by giving you one more night of the most pleasure I can give you before I make my pregnancy my priority. I want you to remember this night for a long time."

"I watched Mary walk toward me taking her clothes off. I was very glad that she had placed the gun on a table as far away as possible. When she reached me she began aggressively removing my clothes. Unfortunately for me, with the shock of seeing a very excited Mary, hearing about the pregnancy, and her intent to have unforgettable sex with me, I had forgotten about Carol."

"I thought I was familiar with Mary's very physical sexual aggressiveness, but her extra excitement was unusual even for her. After she removed my clothes she moved me back onto the bed with her back facing the room entrance door. With Mary on top of me, I was not visible on the bed from six feet or more away. I tried to reposition my body to gain a little more control over my movements. This resulted in a hamstring pull that was causing me very sharp pain, which I was only able to contain for a moment. I could not help yelling out in pain. To Mary, my yells sounded like the yells she and her brothers made when they were at full gallop on their horses riding across the ranch. Mary began shouting encouragement to me to yell louder and 'enjoy the ride!' My yells and her encouragement of joyful free expression fueled her own excitement and resulted in more pain for me."

"I was completely unaware when Carol had returned to the room. She used the key I had given her to open the door and was initially not sure what she was watching when she entered the room. She could not see me and was not sure if the back view of the very large person she could see was a man or a woman."

"Stanley?" Carol said.

"Neither Mary nor I heard her at first. It was when Mary yelled, 'Ride, Stanley, ride!' that she knew I was on the bed, and sounded to her to be in a lot of pain. Not knowing what to do, Carol started yelling, 'Stop! Whoever you are, stop!'"

"Carol's voice was not strong enough to compete with the high-pitched sounds of pain and pleasure coming from Mary and me. Carol started looking around the room and saw Mary's .45-caliber handgun. She lifted the gun from the table with both hands and pointed it toward the far corner from the bed, hoping that if she stopped what was happening on the bed she would find out what was going on. Carol managed to fire the gun into the corner of the room, which did get our attention."

"Mary turned and saw Carol holding her gun."

"Who are you, and what are you doing here, and why did you fire my gun?"

"As Mary got out of the bed Carol called to me and asked what was going on. I couldn't respond to her right away because I was trying to get my breath and hoping for the pain to subside. Mary responded to Carol."

"I don't know who you are, but you have made a big mistake." Mary said. "I'm Mary Oakley, and I am pregnant with Stanley's child, and we are going to be married soon."

"Stanley, is that true?" Carol asked.

"I was still trying to catch my breath and ease the pain in my leg, so it was hard for me to speak. I waved one hand in an effort to get Carol to wait a minute until I could speak. Mary asked Carol again to explain why she had come into the room. Carol explained her relationship with me to Mary. Mary walked over to Carol and took the .45 from her. By this time I had managed to sit on the edge of the bed. My heart sank when I saw Mary take the .45 from Carol. I knew that if Mary fired the gun at me there was no chance that she would miss. I would be a dead man. Mary actually listened very closely to Carol's story and decided that I might possibly have been very honest with her, particularly about my relationship with Carol having no strings attached. Mary walked over to the bed and, without pointing the gun at me, asked me what my intentions were toward her."

"Mary, I have known for a long time that my feelings for you were much stronger than I wanted to admit to myself, and when you told me that you were pregnant I knew I had to do the right thing." I said. "I had been delaying making a decision about our relationship, but I realized that I was in love with you. After learning tonight that you were pregnant, I could not imagine the rest of my life without you and my child. If you would still have me, I would be proud to marry you."

"Stanley, you know I love you, and I will be proud to be your wife," Mary said.

"Thank you, Mary; I'm real glad to hear that," I replied. "After I get some medical attention I will tell you about the rest of my life."

"Howard, boy, shortly after that night I cleared the air with Mary, and we made our wedding plans. I'm making this last train trip to sell my hardware stores in Miami and Detroit and move to Abilene, Texas, as a sign of my commitment to Mary and my child."

"Howard, boy, I've always enjoyed our time together during my train trips. I want you to take this $200 and have a good life. I'll miss seeing you."

"Thank you, boss, I'll miss you too. Good luck to you and your family in Texas."

CHAPTER 10

THE VERNON NEVINS STORY

On a rainy Saturday afternoon in April 1960, Slim Fuller told the story about the day in July 1958 when he and his friend, Jake Shows, met Vernon Nevins at the High Pep gas station. Vernon Nevins was a twenty-five-year-old Negro attempting to drive from Brooklyn, New York, to Biloxi, Mississippi, to visit family members. He was making the trip alone for the first time.

Vernon Nevins was born in the borough of Brooklyn in New York City on March 3, 1933. His parents, Earl and Martha Nevins, were both originally from Biloxi and moved to Brooklyn in 1930. Earl and Martha remained very close to their families in Biloxi after they moved to Brooklyn and wanted their son to share that closeness and heritage. Shortly after his birth, Earl and Martha started an annual tradition of taking Vernon to Biloxi in August. Vernon came to enjoy these annual trips and his family members. However, he was never aware of the protective measures that Earl and Martha took to ensure he was never exposed to the "Jim Crow" South that existed at that time, nor had they ever shared with Vernon the details of some of their more difficult life experiences in that environment. Just before moving to Brooklyn, Earl and Martha told their parents that they had thought long and hard about what kind of life they wanted for themselves and any children they might have in the future. It was a difficult decision given their close ties to family in Biloxi, but they agreed that to provide the best opportunity for a good life for their children and themselves, they would have to leave the South—and soon.

Earl and Martha were classmates since first grade and began dating each other in the ninth grade. By the eleventh grade they were planning their future together and agreed that to have a future they would need to leave the "Jim Crow" South. They graduated high school in May 1929. Earl began working in an auto body repair shop, and Martha worked as a kitchen helper at Biloxi General Hospital. Earl and Martha worked very hard, saved their money, and were married in June 1930. Earl's uncle, John Nevins, who owned his own auto body repair shop, had moved to Brooklyn fifteen years earlier and had purchased a three-story brownstone building in 1928. When Earl told his uncle John that he and Martha would like to come to Brooklyn, John extended a warm welcome and a job in his auto body shop. Earl and Martha moved to Brooklyn in October 1930.

Earl and Martha were elated with the birth of their son, Vernon, in 1933. Vernon was a good student in grade school and graduated high school with a 3.8 grade point average. He attended New York University and received a degree in elementary education. After receiving his degree in 1954, he was hired at the elementary school in his neighborhood in Brooklyn. Earl, Martha, and Vernon loved their annual summer vacation to Biloxi. As he grew older, Vernon took particular pleasure in sharing with his classmates and friends the details of his summer vacations in Biloxi. He was very proud of his parents and his extended family in Biloxi, and they were all very proud of him.

In 1958, after purchasing his first car, a 1958 Ford, Vernon announced to his parents that he would be taking a celebratory extra vacation in July. He would be driving his new car to Biloxi.

"Son, you know we are very proud of what you have accomplished in your life. You have done well, and you are a fine young man, even if it's your parents who say so. We want to ask you to reconsider your trip and wait until we can adjust our schedules to join you. We can help you drive, and, after all, you have never made the trip alone before. It's a lonely drive by yourself. In fact, what might work better is that you wait until August when we usually make the trip together."

"Mom, Dad, I have paid close attention over the years we have made the trip together, and I know I can do it alone safely. Besides, it's time that I prove to myself and to you that I am fully capable of taking care of myself."

"Son, throughout your life we have protected you from the worse side of life in the Deep South. We know that as a teenager and college student you have learned about discrimination, bigotry, and the history of how Negroes have been and are treated in the South, but you have never had any such experiences firsthand. You've had a safe upbringing that builds self-confidence, and we are concerned about how you might respond to discriminatory and racist treatment that is a fundamental basis of life in the South. Your kind of self-confidence, pride, and self-respect could be enough to get you killed."

"I understand what you are trying to tell me, but you don't need to worry because I know that life is different in the South, and I can make the adjustments necessary to survive for one week. This trip will show you that I am capable of facing difficult situations in life and making difficult adjustments. I plan to begin my trip on Saturday morning, July 1, and would start my return trip on Sunday morning, July 10."

Earl and Martha realized that Vernon was not a child any longer, and they would not be able to prevent him from making the journey to Biloxi alone. They said that they would pray for his safe journey and return, and they asked him to call them whenever he could to let them know that he was well.

Vernon prepared well for his trip to Biloxi. He attempted to follow the route that his parents had always taken and to stop at the usual locations for food and rest. His trip had gone well until he reached the Tennessee border with Mississippi. Vernon knew he needed to eventually access Highway 49 to reach Biloxi. However, he would first need to get to Highway 11, which would take him to Highway 49. Leaving Tennessee and crossing into Mississippi, Vernon encountered a major problem. A tractor-trailer truck with a payload of gasoline had struck a bridge and exploded. For safety reasons the highway patrol established roadblocks that required all vehicles to take a two-mile detour to reach local destinations and a five-mile detour to reach another major highway. For Vernon the detour resulted in taking local roads that were poorly identified, if at all. He encountered the detour at about 2:00 p.m. on Sunday.

After about two hours of driving from the detour site, Vernon realized he could not determine from his map how to get to Highway 11, primarily because he could not identify his present location. Part of Vernon's overall travel plan was to avoid unnecessary contact with locals. He now realized he needed help to get back on course. He decided to stop at a gas station to refuel and ask for help. His first stop was at a gas station with one gas pump. He got in line behind the car that was already at the pump. While waiting for the car to move away he noticed that there were only white people in and outside the station. When he saw the car at the pump begin to move away, Vernon prepared to move forward. He then noticed a car in front of the car that was being serviced backing into position at the pump. Vernon was sure that the car backing into position was not there when he arrived at the pump. However, he could not be absolutely sure so he sat quietly and waited for the second car to be serviced. He then saw another car pull up to the other side of the pump. When the second car was finished getting gas, the attendant took the pump around to the other car. Vernon then realized that no one had acknowledged his presence in any way or that he was attempting to get gas. He decided that he would simply leave and look for another gas station.

Vernon traveled about ten miles and found another gas station. However, when he pulled up to the pump he realized that the station was closed. Vernon then remembered that Sundays in the South were considered a day of rest, and all stores were usually closed. He decided to try to find a safe place to rest and hopefully find someone who was willing and able to help him. Vernon drove away from the station slowly and decided that he would conserve his remaining gas and focus on finding help. Around 4:30 p.m. about a mile from the station, he encountered a Negro family of six dressed in their Sunday clothes. Vernon stopped and told the family about his situation and that he needed help to find gas and Highway 11. The gentleman introduced himself and his family to Vernon and invited him to their home for rest, food, and help with his journey.

Vernon had been befriended by Deacon Malcolm Cherry; his wife, Velma; and children, Angela, Betty, James, and Malcolm Jr. He told Deacon Cherry about his experience at the gas station ten miles down the road.

"Son, you made the right decision. If you had not decided to keep quiet and leave, you and I would not be having this conversation. No Negroes are allowed at that gas station. It is for whites only. That is why it is open on Sunday. The only stores that are ever open on Sunday around here serve whites only or Negroes who are on errands for whites. If I were you, whenever I see a store or other place of business where no Negroes are visible, I would leave as soon as possible, especially on Sunday."

Vernon decided to accept Deacon Cherry's hospitality and advice, and spent the rest of the day and night with his family.

The next morning, after a hearty breakfast prepared by Velma, Vernon received careful instruction from Deacon Cherry about how to get to Highway 11. Vernon left the Cherry home at 8:00 a.m. and reached Highway 11 by

8:30 a.m. Getting back to the highway gave Vernon an overwhelming feeling of relief at the thought of being back on track with his journey.

Around 11:00 a.m. Vernon did not feel tired as he was still feeling very happy about being back on his travel course. However, he was in need of a bathroom break. Vernon realized that he was about thirty minutes away from his planned rest stop and could not possibly wait that long. He really needed to stop as soon as he could. About three minutes later Vernon spotted the High Pep gas station with four pumps.

Vernon parked on the side of the station away from the pumps, as he did not need gas at that point. He wanted his stay at this unfamiliar gas station to be as brief as possible. As Vernon got out of his car he saw me and Jake sitting on crates across from the men's room at the station. He thought this was a good sign. At that point he saw a white man exiting the restroom. Vernon then started walking toward the restroom, and he heard us calling him to come over to us.

"I'll come over there after I finish in the restroom."

"You come over here now, not later!"

We yelled kind of loud like we were mad at him to come over to us right then. He looked like a nice kid who probably respected his elders, so we thought yelling at him would make him come right away, and it worked.

"Gentlemen, I don't mean any disrespect, but I need to get to the restroom real bad. I promise I'll come back to talk to you as soon as I finish."

"Son, we yelled at you to make you come over to us quick. Negroes are not allowed to use the restrooms at this gas station under any circumstances. To do so would be to risk life and limb. Such a disregard for the rules would not be overlooked by the station owner or any of the white men you see around here. If you follow us we will show you a location in the bush behind the station where you can relieve yourself."

"Gentlemen, my problem is that I have to do more than urinate, and I need toilet paper."

"Son, there are large leaves in the bush that will work well enough. Your only other choice would be to go another two miles on a side road off the highway where there is a gas station that allows Negroes to use the restrooms."

"Gentlemen, I can't make it another two miles, I don't know if I can make it another two minutes. Maybe if I just went inside the gas station and asked permission they would make an exception."

"Son, the best result you will get from that will be a stern 'no' and an order to get in your car and leave immediately. You will then have to go the additional two miles because they would then not allow you to use the bush. The worse result is that they could hurt you badly or kill you."

"It had to be my luck that I would run into a bunch of backward-thinking rednecks and legal discrimination."

"Son, you have to lower your voice, or all three of us will be in trouble. It will be in all our best interests if you just

JOE DAVID GARNER JR.

went into the bush and got back in your car as soon as possible. The white men in the station will soon notice your out-of-state license plates and know that you are not buying gas."

"Gentlemen, the last thing I want to do is get you two or me in trouble, so I will do as you say."

"Son, be sure to keep your head below the top of the bush to avoid any of the white men throwing soda bottles at you. And don't worry about any small snakes in the grass because they are all green or chicken snakes and not dangerous."

Vernon hesitated a moment and then hurried into the bush. He felt fortunate that no one seemed to notice him, and he did not see any snakes in the bush. When he returned to his car, Vernon thanked us for probably saving his life. Slim gave Vernon his address and asked him to drop him a line when he got to Biloxi. A week later Slim got a letter from Vernon saying that he had arrived in Biloxi safely. He added that when he called his parents to tell them he had arrived safely he said he was glad he made the trip because it had already changed his life forever. Vernon wrote that he told his parents that he would talk to them about the details of his trip and the two helpful old men who saved his life when he returned to Brooklyn.

Slim got a second letter from Vernon after he returned to Brooklyn telling him all about his family and their annual family trip to Biloxi. Vernon wrote that he hoped that his parents could meet us some day on a future trip to Biloxi.

CHAPTER 11

THE WILLIAM WALKER STORY

Green Gillis was sixty-two years old in 1964. In his prime working years from age eighteen to fifty-five, he cut and hauled pulpwood for the Carlston Lumber Company in Bale Hills, Mississippi. Cutting and hauling pulpwood was physically a very difficult and demanding job. At sixty-two, Green Gillis had survived the aches and injuries that are common with pulpwood haulers and still had the body of a thirty-year-old. At six feet and 200 pounds he looked like an Olympic long-distance runner. Green loved to tell the story of William Walker, one of the most financially successful Negroes that he and the other older men in the barbershop had ever personally known. Green knew William best because he worked with him at the lumberyard. Green said he was eighteen years old in 1920 and had been working about two months when William, who was only thirteen at the time, was hired. William Walker was held in the highest regard by every Negro who knew him and was kind of a living legend because of all the obstacles he had overcome on his road to financial success.

William Walker was born in Bale Hills, Mississippi, in 1907. He was the only child born to Saul and Sheba Williams, who were sharecroppers on a one hundred acre farm owned by Leon Wendell in Bale Hills. When he was born, William weighed about twelve pounds, according to the midwife who helped his mother deliver him. It was no surprise when he continued to grow into a larger than usual toddler and adolescent. At age thirteen William was five feet eleven and weighed 180 pounds.

Saul realized that William was about the same size as most of the Negro men and larger than some on the farm and could do as much work. He also knew that Negroes who worked in the logging business made more money than sharecroppers. One night at the dinner table, Saul had a talk with his son and Sheba.

"William, you know that the life of a sharecropper is no more than a means to get by. You can't earn enough money for a future, and there is nothing you can really call yours. God has blessed you with size and strength to do a man's work at the age of thirteen. The only Negroes I know who work and make money that amounts to anything are the loggers. You probably have heard them by the name 'pulpwood haulers.' It's hard work, William, but it has the possibility of a future with some control of your life. I think you are smart enough and strong enough to do logging. Your mama and me are going to spend the rest of our lives on this farm sharecropping and leave this earth with no more than we came with. We won't be able to leave anything for you to help you live. If you are willing, I want to ask Deacon Isaac Washington, who works for the Carlston Lumber Company, to take you with him to ask for a job. If you get a job at the lumber company you will have a chance at a life."

"Son, I think your pa is right. Sharecropping is only for Negroes who have no other choice."

"Okay. I will try."

Deacon Washington was glad to take William to the lumberyard. He introduced William to his boss, Mr. Victor Miland. Mr. Miland was a fair man and a good businessman. He had hired several Negroes who proved to be among his best and most dependable workers.

William was an eager learner. He began work at the lumberyard as an apprentice in 1920, making twenty-five cents per day.

In 1927 at age twenty, William was six feet four and 215 pounds. He had become a full-fledged logger, earning two dollars a day. An imposing but very gentle man, his skin had been darkened over the years from long hours of work in the heat of the Mississippi sun. His body was firm, and his hands were tough as leather. He wore a one-piece coverall, as it was the only garment that gave him the protection and flexibility needed to handle the rough work in the logging industry. His white bosses, particularly Victor Miland, admired his work ethic and desire to learn. They had rewarded him with pay increases and greater responsibility. William knew that no matter what his position, he could never give orders to the white workers in his area. However, this set of circumstances presented no particular difficulties for William. He was proud to have his work recognized and to receive the additional pay.

In 1927 William was able to work out a rental arrangement for a two-bedroom house owned by Victor Miland. He then proposed to Bonnie Simmons, his girlfriend of five years. After the wedding, the couple settled into their new home and began to raise a family. It was always an uphill battle, but William was determined to become his own boss one day, and Bonnie supported his dream 100 percent.

Bonnie was also born in Bale Hills, Mississippi, in 1907. Her parents, Simon and Ester Simmons, were also sharecroppers on Leon Wendell's farm. She and William had known each other since childhood. At age twenty Bonnie was five feet seven and weighed 118 pounds. William said that her skin was the color of coffee with a touch of milk and just as smooth. She had slightly large brown eyes that seemed to sparkle when she laughed. Her hair was black and appeared to be naturally a little straighter than most of the other Negro women. Bonnie always wore her hair in a braid that extended just below her shoulders. There had been some talk when she was born that Leon Wendell might be her father. Over the years her skin became slightly darker but still very smooth.

In 1942, shortly after his thirty-fifth birthday, with the help of Victor Miland, William made a deal with the owners of the company to buy one of their used log trucks for $5,000. It was not the best truck in the world, but it would be good enough to get him started. When William was handed the keys to the truck he felt twice as tall as his six-feet-four frame.

To make his business work, William had to develop a clientele in addition to being able to cut and prepare the logs for delivery. He had learned that there was a special tree, the yellow pine, that customers preferred for the manufacturing of certain products, such as doors, chairs, and tables. This particular wood lasted longer and looked nicer than most others. To get to the yellow pine, William would have to travel 150 miles from his home. It would take him two days to cut and prepare one truckload of logs. He was confident he would succeed. Bonnie helped William prepare for his first trip. She fixed food for a week, packed his work clothes, and made a first aid kit. William would probably have to spend all his time in the woods near his truck unless he happened to meet a friendly Negro family in the area. If he encountered any white people, he would tell them that he worked for the Carlston Lumber Company, and they had sent him out to cut trees. Even though he would not be on private land, he felt this would be acceptable to whites rather than the fact that a Negro man was self-employed.

William made good time and prepared his first log shipment in five days. He proudly drove into the lot of the Carlston Lumber Company and asked to have his shipment inspected. His former boss, Victor Miland, smiled as he inspected the logs.

"William, this is some of the finest yellow pine I have ever seen, and they are cut to perfection. I'm going to sign a purchase order for $600, which you can take to the cashier's window."

"Thank you very much, Mr. Miland. I can't tell you how much I appreciate this. Without your help and support I would not have made it this far."

William was tired but had never felt better in his life. He wanted to celebrate. He stopped at Sally's Restaurant and bought barbecue ribs and fish dinners with all the fixings for the family.

Bonnie and the kids, William Jr., age thirteen, and Ester, age ten, were standing in the front door as they had heard William's truck roll into the yard. He gave everyone a big hug and told them all about his trip. After an enjoyable meal filled with questions from the kids, William gave Bonnie the money he had earned and told her to keep enough to run the house for two weeks. The rest he would take to the bank in the morning. He had planned to make at least two trips per month and did not want much money in the house. Bonnie thought this was a good plan.

As time went on, William was able to expand his clientele to other lumber companies in the state. Negro man or not, they knew quality work when they saw it. William had earned everyone's respect and admiration.

In 1952, at the age of forty-five, William began thinking about when he might turn the business over to William Jr., now twenty-three years old. William Jr. was much smaller than he at five feet nine and 175 pounds and would not be able to handle the heavy work alone. He would need to hire a trustworthy assistant before turning over the business to William Jr. He was beginning to have difficulty loading the logs onto the truck. However, he knew that he would have to develop better business skills if he wanted a staff.

William's next trip was to cut a load of yellow pine for the Anderson Lumber Company in Alp Valley, Mississippi.

He would have to be away from home at least a week. As always, Bonnie prepared everything he would need.

William had found another good location near the Mississippi Delta where the yellow pine was very healthy. He was almost finished loading the freshly cut logs when one of the lift chains broke. William was standing directly under the log. He managed to move his head and torso but the log landed on his right thigh, rolled down his leg, and came to rest on his ankle. William lost consciousness for about twenty minutes. When he awoke he knew his leg was broken. Fortunately, it had rained the past two days, and the ground was soft. After about thirty minutes he was able to dig the earth away around and underneath his ankle with a broken tree limb and slide his foot from under the log. With all his remaining strength, he hobbled to the main road one mile away, where he was picked up by a passerby and taken to a hospital.

William's leg was broken in three places. The doctor informed him that his injuries were so severe that he would not be able to work and would be in a cast for the next four months. William was devastated. William Jr. would not be able to do the work alone, and four months would eat away at his savings. He and Bonnie had managed their money well, but they had no medical insurance. However, being a proud man, William paid all his hospital bills from their savings. He would be able to live from the rest of his savings for a couple of months, but he had to find another source of income as soon as possible.

"William, I will ask around to find out if any of the well-to-do white families need a housekeeper and a yard man. William Jr. will have no trouble doing yard work."

"Thanks, Bonnie. But in the meantime I want you to go to the grocery store and let George Grandy, the owner, know that I would like to speak with him."

George Grandy owned several businesses in town including the grocery store. He was known for his support of segregation but was foremost a businessman. At sixty-one, five feet six, 140 pounds, George Grandy was somewhat paler than most whites in the area. He had always worked inside his father's grocery store, which was passed on to George, and he didn't like the sun.

After explaining to Mr. Grandy what had happened to her husband, Bonnie told him that her husband would like to speak with him on business.

"Mr. Grandy, my husband knows that you are a very busy man but asks that you please try to find a few minutes to stop by our home to talk with him."

"I know about William. He's a good boy. Tell him I'll stop by tonight after the store closes."

"Thank you so much, Mr. Grandy. You are so kind. I will run home and tell William right away."

Mr. Grandy knew William's reputation and respected his hard work. He also knew William had done well with the logging business and had a higher income than most whites in the area. Mr. Grandy believed that it was his responsibility to make sure that William's financial success did not one day pose a problem for the white community. Therefore, this request to speak to him might be a perfect opportunity to make a closer assessment of William's situation.

When Mr. Grandy arrived at the Walker home, Bonnie invited him in and offered him cake and coffee. William was already seated at the kitchen table. William thanked Grandy for coming and offered his hand. Grandy gave a weak handshake in response and sat down at the table.

"You see, Mr. Grandy, my logging accident has rendered me unable to work for at least four months, probably longer, and I want to make sure that my family will not suffer any hardships during this period. Mr. Grandy, I want to ask you if you would extend me credit to purchase food for my family in your store until I can get back to work. As soon as I am able to work again, I will begin repaying my debt to you with whatever interest you feel is right."

Without appearing to give any thought to William's request, Mr. Grandy responded.

"William, don't you worry about a thing, especially food for your family. You will have credit in my store for as long as you need it. William, you are the hardest-working nigger I know. You have always paid your debts. If all the niggers around here were like you, we wouldn't have any problems."

"I don't know how to thank you, Mr. Grandy. This is really a load off my mind. And I do promise to pay you back with interest."

"William, I'm not worried at all. I want you to take these one hundred dollars to use as you feel necessary. If you need anything from any of my stores in town or more money, you just let me know."

"Thank you again, Mr. Grandy."

William was determined to return to his logging work as soon as possible and did so after five months. Immediately after his next logging delivery and over Mr. Grandy's insistence that it was not necessary, he paid Mr. Grandy the $450 for the credit extended to him in Mr. Grandy's grocery store plus $150, including interest, to cover the gift Mr. Grandy had given him shortly after his accident.

William believed that it was important that he paid his debts and particularly not owe special favors to Mr. Grandy or any other white person. A nonmonetary repayment of such a debt as his would sometimes require serving as a maid or a driver at a party and William did not want to subject Bonnie or him to situations where they would be at the mercy of powerful white people.

CHAPTER 12

THE CLEVE JOHNSON STORY

Preacher Casey said that he believed the traveling preacher who had made a note about his birth in the Bible that he gave to his parents. The traveling preacher had a true vision when he told his parents that their son would become a preacher because all his life he had felt a calling from God to speak on the evils of disharmony between Negroes and whites, the wrongs of "Jim Crow" laws, and the powerful influence of the Ku Klux Klan in the South. One of his favorite minisermons at the barbershop was the story of Cleve Johnson.

Cleve Johnson was one of the most successful businessmen and land owners in Dryfield, Mississippi. He was born on November 4, 1905, in Dryfield. In 1945, his father, Grant Johnson, passed away and left Cleve two hundred acres of land and his cotton business. Combined with the occasional sale of land to the state when it started to build more highways, Cleve had solid financial security for himself and his family and was considered to have more power and influence than the Ku Klux Klan. At six feet three and 235 pounds, he was an imposing presence as well.

However, for all his success, he did not bother to take notice of the other very real changes that had taken place around him. His family members, both immediate and extended, while professing their loyalty and devotion to him, were building lives that existed without him. His friends, while expressing their respect and appreciation for him, had come to fear his power and influence and were very afraid of the consequences of arousing his anger. His one expression of affection was to allow everyone to call him "Johnson."

Johnson lived well and in good health until he suffered a massive stroke at age seventy-two. He became bedridden, incontinent, and unable to feed, clean, or dress himself. However, his mind remained amazingly clear, and he was soon able to speak somewhat clearly with effort. When he suffered the stroke, Johnson was certain that his family and friends would take care of him and all his needs. However, he was told by his family after arriving home from the hospital that the amount of care and attention he required would not be possible for them to provide, as they could not afford to ignore their own very important affairs and activities. His wife told him that her role as grandmother now required the majority of her time, and her children depended greatly on her for the care of their children in order that they could carry on with their lives. The family told Johnson to hire someone to care for him. They would see to it that a good person was selected. Feeling somewhat discouraged, Johnson turned to his friends. His friends told him that they didn't have much of their own and simply couldn't afford to give him their time, which they needed to maintain the little they had.

Faced with these shocking revelations from his family and friends, Johnson had to now pay someone to care for him after all his years of service to his family and the white community. Johnson attempted to hire someone in his family to care for him. They all told him that they were not able to do such work, did not have the skills, or just couldn't stand to see him like that. His friends gave him the same reasons for not accepting his offer of employment. As a last resort Johnson placed an ad in the local newspapers. Surely some good white person would want to care for him after all he had done for them. The next day after the ad ran there was a knock at his door. It was Ida Jones, a forty-year-old Negro female inquiring about the job. Johnson told his temporary nurse from the hospital, who came by each day for an hour to give him his medications, change his adult diaper, and give him a sponge bath, to send the nigger away, as he would only allow a white person to care for him. One of his own would be responding to the ad soon enough. The nurse thanked Ms. Jones for responding to the ad and told her that the position had been filled. Ms. Jones thanked the nurse and asked her to take a piece of paper with her name, address, and telephone number in case the nurse knew of similar employment opportunities.

Days passed, and then weeks, with no other responses to his ad. When Johnson's hospital nurse had only four days left to spend with him, as a last effort he called in two of his farm crew bosses, Elmer Griss and Lloyd Grims. He asked them to go to Long Bow, Tennessee, the home of his deceased parents where the Johnson name has been respected for many years and find someone to care for him. Johnson told them they had three days to accomplish their goal. They promised to do their best to find someone.

Three days later the two men reported back. They had almost knocked on the door of every white family in Long Bow but could not locate anyone wanting or willing to accept Johnson's job offer. Upon hearing the news, Johnson felt for the first time in his life a sense of helplessness and despair. His nurse from the hospital offered to contact Ida Jones. Johnson only waved his hand slightly and nodded his head affirmatively. The nurse then called Ms. Jones and told her Johnson was again seeking someone to care for him, as the previous person had to leave town for personal reasons. Ms. Jones said yes to the offer. The nurse felt compelled to caution and prepare Ms. Jones for what she might face with Johnson, both in regard to his physical needs and his lifelong commitment to white supremacy. Ms. Jones told the nurse that everyone in town as well as the state knew all about Cleve Johnson. However, she needed employment badly, and the money was better than any other job that she would be able to get.

The next day was spent with the nurse instructing Ms. Jones about all aspects of Johnson's care. All went well, as Ms. Jones had had nurse's training in the past. The nurse from the hospital told Johnson that she was very impressed with Ms. Jones. Johnson did not respond. Nor did he respond at the end of the day when the nurse was saying good-bye. Johnson seemed to be using all his emotional energy to somehow accept the reality of his loss of independence; the nonresponsiveness of his family and friends, and most of all, having to be cared for by a nigger.

In the beginning, Johnson seemed to draw more and more within himself and appear not to notice the presence of Ms. Jones. However, he could not ignore for long the quality of care Ms. Jones was giving him. She always had a smile and an encouraging word for Johnson. She never complained when he had "accidents" while she was changing his adult diaper. She inquired about his favorite foods and cooked them often with a new and better taste than Johnson remembered.

The weeks turned into months. Johnson began to look forward to seeing Ms. Jones each morning and the delicious breakfast she always prepared for him. Somehow, his life had begun to have a new meaning. He first began to analyze Ms. Jones to see if she was indeed as genuine a person as she seemed. Johnson quickly realized that she was completely sincere and would continue to give him the best of care regardless of how long and frequently he spoke of the virtues of the white race and the need for niggers to stay in their place. He asked her one day why she always seemed happy. Ms. Jones told him that she had many problems to deal with, but God was good, and she knew, as has always been the case, that He would make everything right. Johnson, to his surprise, began to question his own life and beliefs.

One morning Ms. Jones came into Johnson's room to find him crying uncontrollably. After several minutes of trying to calm him down and checking him thoroughly to locate any physical cause of pain, she managed to get Johnson to respond regarding the source of his discomfort. Johnson told her he had now come to realize that most of his lifelong beliefs and ideals were completely wrong. He told Ms. Jones that until he met her, he had never met anyone who truly understood God's message of love for mankind and His desire for us to love one another. Johnson told Ms. Jones that from the moment he became ill it was painfully obvious that those closest to him knew nothing of God's message of love—and neither did he.

"Ida, in the time I have left in this world I want to try to make amends for the wrong things I have done, and especially for my hatred of colored people. Tell me, what should I do?"

"Mr. Johnson, all I can tell you is to ask God's forgiveness and guidance. Listen and He will direct you."

Over the next couple of months, Johnson made arrangements to ensure financial security for Ida and her family and rewrote his will to exclude all support for the Ku Klux Klan and its activities. Johnson was visited by several family members and friends who tried to convince him that the feelings he had would pass and that he should not alter his commitment to white supremacy. Johnson did not listen to their pleas. Until his death a year later, he continued to give money to causes important to the Negro community, and he continued his proclamation of God's love for everyone.

CPSIA information can be obtained at www.ICGtesting.com
Printed in the USA
LVOW080125060313

322898LV00001B/16/P

9 781475 922424